The Madman of Icchapurti

Sucheta RK

notionpress.com

INDIA · SINGAPORE · MALAYSIA

'So, my brothers and sisters, remember, that to feed a hungry creature is a virtuous act. God is in each one of us, in all His creations. Every time you feed a hungry mouth, human or otherwise, you repay a debt long overdue. Nothing is more pleasing to God than to be fed through the mouth of a poor hungry creature. Tonight on your way home from the satsang, remember my words when you see a stray dog. Remember my words when a hungry crow comes calling tomorrow at your kitchen window. Yes, my children, if you see a man feed and serve a helpless creature, bow to him for that is how God wishes you to be. God be with you tonight on your way home. Bless you all. Om.'

And folding his hands in a gesture of leave taking, Vijay Prasad reverently closed the holy book in front of him, slowly stretched his rheumatic knees and gently straightened himself to his full stature. The people of Ichhapurti waited respectfully for him to move away from the seat under the banyan tree, where he delivered his weekly sermon on the holy books, before wending their way home. Vijay Prasad was the younger brother of Devi Prasad, the richest Brahmin of Ichhapurti.

The motley crowd that had gathered for the sermons included Devi Prasad's thirteen-year-old son, Birju, and his friends Hari and Kedar. Birju, Kedar and Hari sat in rapt attention all through the sermon, which was not always the case. But only yesterday Birju's Father Devi Prasad (undoubtedly with some prodding from Birju's sermon-delivering but otherwise liberal-minded Uncle, Vijay Prasad) had arranged a trip to the cinema for the three boys. It was a totally unexpected development given Devi Prasad's aversion to anything remotely modern and in the boys' eyes, merited at least an attendance, albeit reluctant, at the sermon.

'Well, well,' Birju whispered to his friends. 'Looks like our obeisance to Deja is long overdue.'

'What do you mean?' Kedar queried.

'Didn't you hear my Uncle?' Birju answered. 'If you see a man feed and serve a helpless creature, bow to him. As far as I recollect, Deja is the only one in Ichhapurti who refuses to eat before feeding his dog.'

Hari giggled at Birju's words. 'Don't let anyone hear you, Birju. If they do, your Father and Uncle will skin you alive. And we can forget about the cinema.'

That was true. For, Deja was better known as the madman of Ichhapurti. The three boys were the only ones who referred to him by name. For everyone else he was simply the madman of Ichhapurti, which of course, meant he was probably the sanest man there. Madman was simply a label conferred by a community that had unjustly condemned him to a solitary life in the woods behind the village. The whole village had convicted Deja (unfairly, Birju knew for certain) on the charge that he had dared, not only to enter the premises of a Brahmin, but had intended to kill him with the objective of robbing his house.

Their village, like so many all over the country, was divided on caste lines. As a Brahmin boy, what Birju studied in the holy books seemed clear to him. Brahmin, Kshatriya, Vaishya and Shudra were four different categories of men. One who was inclined to study, to works of the intellect, in ancient times inclined towards study of the scriptures and hence, the safeguarding of society's moral and spiritual sanctity, was a Brahmin; the man robust enough and willing to physically defend his nation and his community was a Kshatriya, ready to be a warrior; the man who could run a successful trade and understood the essence of money, was a Vaishya. The Shudra was anyone who did not fit into any of the above categories, which included farmers, artisans, laborers and others who were considered ideal nominees for so-called lesser jobs. Among the shudras themselves, the lowest of the low, the ones who carried out menial work that no one else was willing to do, soon found themselves categorized as untouchables, shunned by the higher castes and outcasts among their own. Down the ages, though the upper castes would not admit it, heredity had staked its unearned claim upon the caste system. Where intrinsic ability had been the only requisite, now the accident of birth was sole criterion. While the erosion of the principle of merit altered little in the lives of the upper castes, it presaged eternal damnation of the shudra.

Adversity of birth had relegated Deja to this last class, though in conduct Birju considered him no less than his peer. Unfortunate circumstances had condemned Deja to a solitary life, in what was called the unholy woods that ringed the village to its south. Though he was permitted entry into the village outskirts, he was barred from entering the main streets of Ichhapurti. The main streets of the village had one thing in common. They were home to Ichhapurti's Brahmins and other upper caste, wealthy Kshatriya and Vaishya families. They were the ones who ensured that Deja's shadow would never darken their streets ever again.

Birju, Hari and Kedar remembered that day like it was only yesterday.

There was great excitement in the village that evening, six months ago. Under the banyan tree in the village grounds, where Birju's Uncle held his discourse the whole village gathered. Never had anyone dreamed that something like this could ever happen. That a man from the low caste would dare to defile a Brahmin with his touch! Unthinkable! And to consider that the victim was none other than Vishnudev, Ichhapurti's most revered Brahmin. Who had presided over almost every one of Ichhapurti's births and deaths, and conducted more religious rites than anyone cared to remember. Birju, Hari and Kedar were there too. They were excited at first, but their excitement soon soured into a strange unease. Under the tree, were seated the men of Ichhapurti who would decide Deja's fate. The rest of the village arranged itself in front of them, some of them standing in groups, some stretched out on the ground in anticipation of a long innings. Deja squatted at some distance beyond the tree, the men who would decide his fate with their backs to him. There was something about him that reminded Birju of a hounded animal. His very posture spoke of hopelessness and despair, and his eyes conceded resignation. This was not a man who was going to put up a fight. Indeed, as an untouchable his chances of being heard were practically nil. The men had earlier held a private hearing with Deja. If you could call it private. Since he was an outcast and the others wouldn't go anywhere near him, the private hearing was actually held at this very place, with a crowd of selected onlookers. The only thing Birju was sure of, was the distance between the two sides. The untouchables had to maintain a distance of about fifteen feet from people of the other castes and when you are in dire need of being heard, fifteen feet can make all the difference in the world. Now the self-appointed judges were to present their case to the people of Ichhapurti and announce their verdict.

'My dear brothers,' Birju's Father, Devi Prasad began. 'Today is a day of disgrace and dishonor for Ichhapurti. For generations, as far back as the oldest Brahmin in Ichhapurti can remember, our village has been a model for others to follow. We have had a proud tradition of serving the less fortunate, in whom God says we must acknowledge Him. For ages, have our Fathers and our forefathers upheld the vision of equality among God's children. We have looked after the lower castes as our own people, even allowing them the privilege to walk the main streets of our village square. But today,' Devi Prasad's voice soared with emotion at the impending accusation, 'today, our long tradition of compassion and caring has been abused. Today, a person from the lower caste has dared to breach the ancient laws of community. I cannot even bring myself to speak of it, suffice to say that an untouchable has committed the unthinkable crime. And it shows him in even poorer light to reflect that he chose as his intended victim, Ichhapurti's most beloved man, the honorable Vishnudev.'

The crowd murmured its approval of the esteem bestowed on the alleged victim. Birju and his friends listened in rapt attention. They could feel the pulse of the crowd, the edginess with which they awaited the inevitable judgment. Some of them considered this gathering a waste of time and were not averse to voicing their disgust. 'Get done with him,' some growled. 'Why all this furor for a shudra? Stone him to death and hold him up as an example to his clan.' This was new to the boys, in their lifetime at least there had never been anything like this. This was their first taste of the village justice system.

'But what has he done?' Kedar whispered to his friends.

'I don't really know,' Birju said. 'I heard snatches of what these people were saying. Seems like Deja tried to kill the fat old man by pushing him into the well.' The boys had a great dislike for Vishnudev and always referred to him as the Fat Old Devil. They were not alone. Most children in the village instinctively avoided Vishnudev. He had little to say to them. When he did condescend to notice the children, it was only to curse their existence and the severe tirade almost succeeded in inspiring guilt in his juvenile victims for emerging in his line of vision.

'Would have served him right, you know,' Birju continued, and his friends looked at him in admiration. Birju always spoke his mind. 'The only accusation I can think of foisting on poor Deja's head is, of trying to poison Ichhapurti's groundwater by drowning the Fat Old Devil in it – and failing,' he added. Hari and Kedar giggled.

'That's true,' Hari smiled. 'But *Deja*? He wouldn't hurt a fly. Who could have thought of it?'

'The Fat Old Devil, who else? His well isn't even ready as yet. If Deja did indeed have the intellect to choose a watery grave for the fat old man, I'm sure he's also equipped with the common sense to appreciate that a large body of water was crucial. I've seen the well; you couldn't drown in it if you tried.'

'But that means,' Kedar chimed in, 'that they are *lying*!'

'So? Is this the first time you've come across a lie?'

'But Birju… that is your Father there telling us all about it.'

'And there's *your* Father, Kedar, valiantly proposing we do away with Deja immediately.'

'But…but Birju, how can they lie? They are…we're… we're – '

'We are – they are Brahmins. Are they not?' Birju whispered fiercely through gritted teeth.

'Y…Yes.'

'Swear upon God that you've never uttered a lie, Kedar. Do it. I dare you to.'

'Well…I do lie…Only now and then. But they're usually about small things, Birju. Mostly stealing mangoes, or saying I've studied when I haven't.'

'So if you are a young Brahmin and can utter a lie, what's to stop *them*? They are better than us – at everything.'

'But they are grownups, Birju,' Hari interceded. 'They don't lie.'

'Really? When you finally grow up, you'll see that your eyes and nose and arms and legs are not the only things that are growing with you. As far as I can see, the older you grow the more you lie. It comes effortlessly, too.'

'How do you know all this, Birju?'

'Because, I make it my business to study people. When somebody says something to me, you can be sure I'll doubt first and believe later. *If* and when I'm convinced. Don't you people ever use your brains? Next time you sit down to study the scriptures, do yourself a favor and try to really understand what's said. Then look around you and see if people live their lives according to the injunctions laid out.'

Birju frowned at the boys and his friends sensed his thoughts moving off at a tangent. The boy could not believe his friends' naïveté. 'Of course,' he thought to himself. 'I'm blessed with the added advantage of having the village guru for my Uncle. One who swears freely in the presence of the lower castes and intones blessed mantras for the benefit of more sensitive ears.'

Birju was witness to man's tendency for duplicity at close quarters. 'One must care for the underprivileged as one does for a child. There is nothing that pleases God more,' the village guru extolled at the weekly sermon. Village guru, aka Birju's Uncle Vijay Prasad, however, was free of any obligation to please God when he flung the copper mug at his servant if the temperature of the bath water was not right.

'Wealth, like blood, must keep circulating for a healthy life. The more you give, the more you get, because God likes balance and He is always watching.' And the village guru would smile benignly at his audience. Presumably, God was busy elsewhere, when Vijay Prasad withheld fifty rupees and five hundred grams of rice from his illiterate servant's wages for unsanctioned leave, when in mathematical fairness, he should have deducted only fifteen rupees and two hundred grams, if at all from the poor man.

Birju had once complained to his Father about his Uncle's blatantly incongruous actions and for an answer, had received memorable pearls of wisdom. 'As long as you are not the victim of his misappropriation, close your eyes and your ears. And unless you are in desperate need of a thrashing, mind your own business.' After that, to all appearances Birju went about with eyes and ears closed – but an open mind.

The village meeting proceeded as expected. Deja was convicted of attempting to take a Brahmin's life with the intent of robbing him. Vishnudev was extolled as the very incarnation of love and mercy. For he had gallantly forgiven his would-be-assassin. In fact, when it was announced that the elders had reached a decision to keep Deja confined to the unholy woods behind the village and to bar him from the main streets of Ichhapurti, the fat old man had come forward and offered to feed Deja once a day since he could no longer be employed. There were more cries of approbation from the audience, for some of the good karma of Vishnudev was sure to rub off on the village as a whole.

To add insult to Deja's injury, his own community refused to have anything to do with him. Deja, it seemed, had brought shame to them. As if the daily intrinsic humiliation of being an untouchable was not enough, he had now gone and got himself entangled in a disgraceful situation. Deja tried his best to clear his name within his community, but there is something to be said for the power of words. The untouchable has for so long, through so many ages endured the insult of being written off as a liar, and being unjustly labeled everything, from lazy to worthless to little more than a beast of burden, that he no longer suspects the truth of those words. Deja did not stand a chance. Even in his own hamlet, Vishnudev's Brahmin tongue carried more weight than Deja's faultless character. In the end, it was Deja's own people who deprived him of his only solitary possession; his sense of identity and belonging.

Deja was condemned to spend the rest of his life in the woods behind the village. Though he would be allowed into the village, it was generally understood that a sense of shame (if a low caste could bring himself to feel anything like that) would prevent him from doing so. He was to keep away from the main streets and if ever he was seen even attempting to talk to anyone in Ichhapurti, he would be stoned to death. If it had not been for Vishnudev, the man he had allegedly tried to kill, he would certainly have starved to death, for the unholy woods nurtured nothing that could sustain an adult for even a few days.

❧

Back home, sleep eluded Birju. The scene at the grounds haunted him. After the verdict had been announced and approved of by the crowd, Deja, who all along had squatted in silence with his arms crossed over his knees stood up slowly, folded his hands in the direction of Vishnudev and simply turned and walked away in the direction of the woods. The crowd stood watching and Birju felt his hair stand on end as he immediately recognized the dignity with which Deja was conducting himself. He had not been given a fair trial. In fact, for all they cared he was already in the woods. He had sat, listened and walked away without a word of protest, knowing that protesting his innocence would only invite the ire of the villagers. *That* was what they wanted all along, that was what they had come to witness. A groveling, begging shudra, somehow, reinforced their superior status and reassured them of their formidable rectitude. Deja knew he was innocent. That was all that mattered. None of the people gathered here mattered in any way. It was his misfortune that they directed the course his life would take. But that was all he would allow them. As an untouchable, they could tell him what road to walk on. *How* he walked on that road was totally up to him. And though Birju was only thirteen at the time, he readily acknowledged in Deja's conduct something that commanded admiration. As he watched the receding figure, he felt a baffling yet deep and righteous desire rise up in his heart, to stand up and applaud him for he knew not what. As he grew up in a cruel world he would look back on this moment and understand why that urge to applaud has arisen. He was too young now to comprehend, but not too young to feel a sense of respect for the unhappy desolate man, who had so indubitably proved that man is capable of retaining the last vestiges of his dignity in the most humiliating of circumstances.

That night, at least one person in Ichhapurti had behaved like a man.

And then, it arrived. That which Birju's as yet unworldly eyes readily recognized as worthy of admiration, the crowd deemed an affront to its dignity. They had expected tears, pleas for mercy, begging and beseeching. They had not come to see justice being done. Indeed, justice was the last thing on their minds. They had come to ogle at a poor impoverished creature, admit his unworthiness, to watch as he pleaded and prayed before them for mercy. And none of it had come forth. All this precious time wasted – for what? So that they could come and watch an untouchable turn his back on them? Something that the crowd had been expecting, eagerly anticipating, had been snatched away by a destitute. They had been cheated of something elusive but crucial – almost vital – to their very image as people of a higher order. Deja may have been wrongly convicted of attempted murder and robbery, but he had truly turned thief now. He had robbed the beast of its prey. In fact, he had conducted himself like a true Brahmin. But they would not let him carry away the honors so easily. Someone called him a name, but Deja trudged along his path without as much as looking back. Then some of the men picked up stones and hurled them in his direction. When even that did not elicit any response, someone remarked that it was a waste of time to bother with a madman. And at last, unearthing something with which to mask its recently inflicted sense of deprivation, the crowd laughed out loud in agreement and Deja was never known by his name again.

That night, tossing and turning restlessly in bed, Birju got up with the intention of going to his Mother. Mother was different from everyone else. In fact, Birju's sensitive side was a gift from his Mother. Often he watched as his Mother reimbursed a servant who had been wrongfully cheated by the men of the house. She didn't offer it as compensation, for that would mean admitting to a fault in her family and Mother would never do that. But she would set them an easy task and then surprise them with a handsome remuneration.

He had seen Mother soothe their intangible wounds at being publicly rebuked for a minor fault, with her kind words. Mother was an ocean of peace and joy. Nothing and no one was too small or trivial for Mother. She would calm the storm raging in his heart.

As he was passing through the corridor outside his Father's room, he stopped as he heard him in conversation with Vijay Prasad. 'That Vishnudev is a fool,' he heard his Father say. 'It's a good thing both of us were there at the scene or it would have been very difficult to convince the others.'

Birju smiled at his Father's words. He had called the Fat Old Devil a fool; at least there they were in agreement. 'I could barely hold my tongue there, in Vishnudev's courtyard when I saw the two of them. What a sight!' Vijay Prasad's laughter rang out loud and raucous.

'Serves the old fool right. Imagine what a blow it must be to him. Ichhapurti's purest Brahmin, calling out to a shudra to save his life!'

'That too when he's already got one foot planted in the grave,' Birju's Father replied.

'If that shudra had any real sense he'd have done a neat job of kicking him into the well,' Vijay Prasad continued. 'Oh well, we must not be too covetous. Since it's an open secret that he was in actual touch with that madman, we can expect at least half his clients to avail our unsullied services.'

'But we've lost a good worker. Deja may be mad,' Birju's Father was saying, 'but he was a most uncomplaining worker. Never got it into his head that he could finish today's job tomorrow. Did you see his face, when Vishnudev came up with that yarn of how he had been pushed into the well?'

'Good thing Vishnudev collected his wits about him quickly. Or else he wouldn't have been able to face any of us. As it is, we have something on him now. Don't think he'll try to embellish his well-worn, 'Pedigree-Brahmin-of-Ichhapurti' title as usual, seeing that we know he called to the madman for help. That's a handy sword to hang over his head.' And the two men laughed at the thought of Ichhapurti's most pious Brahmin hanging feet up, down the side of the well.

Outside the door Birju stood rooted to the spot, shocked at the thought that his suspicions had turned out to be true. Vishnudev had actually fallen in and called out to whoever was passing by. He had recognized Deja and had fairly bullied the man to come in and save him. And poor Deja had done as he was told, as he had done all his life. And how had he been rewarded? With abuses and stones, and a lifetime of isolation.

Back in his room, Birju sat by the window and the picture of Deja's receding figure kept coming back to him. He fought to keep back his tears as he thought back to what he had once read in the scriptures: To kill a Brahmin was the worst sin a man could incur. Then surely to save a Brahmin must count as an act of merit? Then why did Deja have to suffer? He knew that all over the world, scriptures were manipulated by powerful people for their own ends. These were the people who swore by the holy books and their tenets. Did their conduct then reveal the limitation of the scriptures, or were their acts to be construed as a moral caveat for what the scriptures could do to man? And how could his Father be a party to such an act? He knew his Father was only as human as his Uncle, but was he so inhuman as to let an innocent man suffer for the fault of another?

A thousand thoughts battled for attention in his mind. What was that primeval pleasure that grownups seemed to eagerly anticipate, almost perversely relish, in degrading another human life? What was it, in Deja's supremely dignified conduct that had threatened their very superior sense of self? Did good and bad, virtue and sin trade places as people grew up? Was all the honesty and integrity, love and patience, inculcated in – nay – almost demanded of childhood, simply to be abandoned in the freewill of adulthood?

'Poor Deja,' Birju thought. And as the picture of him walking away came back to him, he put his hands over his eyes, trying to shake the image out of his mind. Somewhere inside the little boy, among all the disconcerting thoughts, an agonizing voice staked its claim. Surely, by electing to be a part of the crowd he had emerged as a partner in the crime?

❦

Hari and Kedar could not believe their ears.

'Are you sure you did not dream the whole thing?' Kedar asked. The three boys were in the chikoo grove that belonged to Hari's Father, under a tree that generously spread out its branches offering cool respite from the blazing sun. Somewhere in the tree, a little bird chirped as she fed her little offspring. Normally the boys would have stuffed themselves with the sweet fruit, but today the bounty lay untouched. Birju had told them what he had heard the night before. And both the boys were aghast at the news. Even though they readily admitted that grown-ups seldom indulged in the kind of behavior they demanded from their children, both Hari and Kedar had reservations about how far their elders would go in condemning an innocent man. Kedar, though a trusty comrade, was given to fits of weakness in the face of his friend's almost alarming forthrightness. Kedar was the first to admit that Birju never lied, but he drew the line at accusing his own family. Even Hari, who never doubted Birju's integrity, was circumspect. Birju brushed aside their cynicism with a wave of his hand.

'Kedar,' he said. 'Just close your eyes for a moment.'

Kedar did as he was told.

'Imagine you are bathing in the river and suddenly a swift current sweeps you along and you're unable to swim to the banks. Are you ready?'

'Give me a minute Birju,' Kedar responded. 'All that imagining takes time.'

'Now,' Birju asked, after about ten seconds.

'Okay.'

'Now as you're being swept away you see someone walking along the banks, are you going to waste time wondering if the man is an untouchable or otherwise? Or are you going to call out for help?'

Kedar sat still with his eyes closed.

'Speak up, Kedar,' Birju prodded him. 'Does life mean so little that you are willing to die rather than risk the touch of an untouchable?'

'No,' Kedar answered, eyes still shut tight. 'I wouldn't care who it was, as long as he saved my life.'

Birju shook him by the shoulder. 'Open your eyes now. Do you believe the Fat Old Devil values his life any less than you value yours?'

'But Deja wouldn't dream of opening his mouth.' Hari intervened. 'Why didn't he just ask Deja not to say a word about it to anybody?'

'Because the others, including my Father and my Uncle were already on the scene. You don't expect the Fat Old Devil to admit that he called out to Deja for help, do you? He'd rather die than sully his image as supreme Brahmin of Ichhapurti. He put the blame on Deja to save his own skin, to stop being ridiculed in his own community. Can't you see, both of you? People like him make a living out of preaching purity and piety, and denouncing the shudras for being the most tainted creatures on the face of the earth. To acknowledge that he called on one of 'the tainted' to save his life would be worse than death itself.'

Silence greeted this speech from Birju. In the quiet chikoo grove the birds sang and the squirrels scampered about, blissfully ignorant of the tumult in the lives of the three boys. And in those quiet moments, lonely Deja had made three new friends for life.

They were careful not to be seen on their way to the woods. Deja was reluctant to speak with them at first. He thought they had come to ridicule him. When he realized they meant well, he feared what would happen if anyone saw them. If ever the villagers found out. But Birju dispelled those fears, saying even the path to the woods was never used because it was linked to the unholy woods.

Birju asked him about the stray dog that lay next to him. 'Oh, I call him Bittu,' Deja said, passing his hand in a caress over the lean sand colored dog that thumped its tail on the ground and raised its ears at his touch. 'He followed me all the way here the night I was banished. He's been my only friend. I've tried to make him go away, but he won't leave my side.'

'What does he eat?'

'Whatever I do.'

'What do you eat, Deja?'

'Master's servant leaves a plate of food near the trees there, where the path ends. A couple of rotis, and a little vegetable.'

'Once a day?'

'Once a day.'

'And you share that with Bittu?'

'I give him a little food, he gives me all his time,' Deja smiled. 'He's poorer for the bargain.'

The boys looked at each other. Two rotis, and a little vegetable. Even they, as kids, needed a lot more than that in one meal. And Deja and his dog shared that once a day. They looked at the lean figure, squatting with his arms crossed over his knees. The first day he had spoken with them, he had drawn a line on the ground with a broken twig.

'This is your lakshman rekha,' he had said. 'Neither of us must cross this. You speak with me from the other side and I'll answer from here.'

Even now in the isolation of the woods his sense of ignominy had not left him.

After drawing the line for the first time, Deja went back a good distance and sat on the ground. Birju beckoned him closer.

'No,' Deja called out. 'That's too close to get to me.'

'Deja, if you sit so far away we'll have to yell out to each other and then someone's sure to hear us.'

That brought Deja closer to the line. The boys smiled to see the dog trail him like a shadow. Deja always squatted in the same fashion. Down on his haunches, his arms wrapped around his knees.

The first day there was hardly any conversation. None of the boys knew what to say. Deja was the embodiment of concision and rarely spoke, except in response to a question.

Initially, they went almost every afternoon, when most people in the village stayed indoors and slept to avoid the heat. But Deja refused to see them every day. 'You don't understand the enormity of what you are doing. I will not come to see you. It will only cause you unnecessary trouble. Come once a week if you must.'

And he had stuck to his word. When the boys had called out to him in the subsequent days, he refused to emerge from the woods. But he relented a few days later and then the boys agreed to come once in five days. As the days passed, it was easier for them to relate to each other. The three friends felt a sense of obligation in their trips to Deja. Somehow it made them feel better and then, the fact that what they were doing was dangerous injected a sense of adventure into their otherwise routine lives. But more than anything else what gave them the greatest pleasure was the knowledge that Deja actually looked forward to their visits. Even if they spent some days with hardly a word between them, they knew the man was happy. It showed in his eyes, and the awkward words of gratitude he murmured when their time was up. Some days, they brought him fruits, on others food siphoned off from their kitchens. The boys would leave it on the line drawn on the ground and Deja would lift the leaf plate and divide the food into two portions, watching as his dog devoured his portion in seconds. Deja himself never ate in the boys' presence.

'It will be an insult to you,' he told the boys one day and Birju had flown into a rage.

'Deja!' he exploded. 'You are a human being. For God's sake do not insult the almighty by belittling his creation. Your *dog* can eat in front of us, but you deny yourself the right to do the same. Are you worse than the animals then?'

'Do not be angry, Birju baba,' Deja replied. 'A dog is after all a dumb creature, so we have an obligation to look after it. And what does it understand of the ways of the world? But, I can at least think for myself. I have been brought up to always come last, to give way. There are some things I must deny myself.'

'But why will you not *eat* in our presence?

'Because it will be an affront to your dignity.'

He said it with such compelling simplicity and sincerity that for a moment the boys almost believed it. But, on Birju, the effect of the words was devastating. The little boy drew himself up to his full height, clenching his fists.

'Deja! Will you ever dispute a Brahmin's word?'

'I would not dream of it.'

'Then get your food and eat it, Deja,' Birju commanded. 'Here, in front of us.'

Deja stared at the boy as if he was seeing a ghost. He opened his mouth to say something then decided against it. But he didn't move from his perch.

'Deja!' Birju almost shouted. 'Will you dare defy the word of a Brahmin?'

Deja folded his hands in a gesture of supplication. 'It is not in me to defy anybody, Birju baba. Do not think of it as a refusal. You are still only a small child with a big heart, innocent of the ways of the world. For once, allow me the freedom to think for myself.'

Hari and Kedar looked on in horror at Birju, who had begun trembling with every word that he spat out through clenched teeth.

'Deja, people like you will never know what freedom means.' Birju's voice rose with his ire. 'Think for yourself, did you say? Pray, do not deceive yourself. If this line on the ground is as far as your thinking will take you, Deja, then I hope you rot here till you die.' And abruptly turning away to hide the angry tears that took him by surprise, Birju ran as fast as his trembling legs could carry him, leaving three very startled people behind.

Hari and Kedar looked at each other and then at Deja. 'Don't mind him, Deja,' Hari volunteered. 'Birju can be a little hot tempered sometimes. He doesn't mean what he says when he is angry.'

'Don't worry, Hari baba. I know he means well. Go to him now, I'll be alright.'

The boys got up, the silence still an awkward presence between them.

Deja stood up, folded his hands in his usual gesture of gratitude and watched along with Bittu as the two boys turned and walked away.

The boys met in the chikoo grove the next day, Birju much more subdued after a good night's sleep. They avoided the topic all afternoon and spent their time playing cricket and climbing trees. When their energy was spent they lay down on the soft grass in the shadow of the trees.

'Were you guys there for a long time, after I left?' Birju asked.

'Not really,' Kedar answered. 'We left almost at once.'

'Did he… did he say anything?'

'No,' Hari answered. 'He said he understands. But you must learn to hold your tongue, Birju. Sometimes you're worse than the grownups.'

'I know,' Birju admitted. 'But how can he degrade himself like that? Do you remember how he reacted so calmly before the crowd? Only a strong man can do that. And yet see how he talks!'

'Yes,' Hari said. 'But I think you went about it in the wrong manner. Granted, Deja will never do anything that can get us into trouble, nor defy any of us. But you also forgot that acceding to a Brahmin's unusual request has landed him where he is today. Show some common sense, Birju. You cannot bully a man into a new way of thinking.'

'I know. I wish now I hadn't spoken so unkindly.'

That was what was good about Birju. He was hot tempered and sometimes brutally forthright and outspoken, but he was also gracious enough to admit his follies.

On their next visit, Deja, apparently oblivious of the fact that he was a shudra, continued to conduct himself like a Brahmin of the highest order. He professed total ignorance of the one-sided altercation of the past week, taking recourse to a sudden bout of amnesia and politely refusing Kedar's offer to reinvigorate his memory.

Slowly, over the course of a few months, Deja's natural reticence gave way to a shy candidness. Like the flower buds, awaiting the coming of the sun to launch into full bloom, so Deja awaited the boys' visits. Though he spoke little and then only with some encouragement, the joy he felt upon seeing them was palpable. He once said that even Bittu could tell the day on which the boys were to arrive. Bittu, he said, kept looking in the direction from where the boys came. Slowly, he confided in the boys (upon being asked), about the episode with Vishnudev.

They liked to hear the story from Deja himself. There was something funny, yet sad, in the way he narrated the incident to the boys. But even in their young minds they understood that the sadness didn't derive from what he had suffered since then (indeed, he stoutly rubbished the very idea of his suffering), it ensued from a genuine inability on his part to comprehend what he had done wrong. And yet, in spite of this, he had accepted the treatment meted out to him by the villagers. When Birju argued on his behalf he would wave a bony hand in the air and say, 'I don't understand where I erred, so how can you expect me to sit on judgment over the punishment? And then, they know more than me. After all, I am only an untouchable.'

Deja's story was unwavering in content. As far back as he could remember, he had worked for Vishnudev's family. His Father, grandFather, and probably everybody before them had worked for the same family. He remembered trudging the distance from his home to that of Vishnudev's, as a child. Vishnudev had been a strapping young man then, the apple of the Ichhapurti Brahmin community's collective eye. As a rule, the Brahmin community considered themselves above all the other castes, but that didn't stop them from admiring Vishnudev's Kshatriya like robust frame. In this village, like in so many across this vast country, people rigidly followed caste lines. And as Deja had the misfortune of being born into the caste commonly known as the Harijans or untouchables, he had begun life's journey on the wrong side. 'But there is a bright side to that, you know,' he told his juvenile audience. 'Once you are born into this community, anything else that occurs is mere happenstance. Look at me, I can take anything in my stride. Imagine if anything like this were to happen, God forbid, to someone from the village, he would have taken his own life.' His childhood days had never varied. He accompanied his Father as a young boy to Vishnudev's house every morning. Vishnudev's 'house' was a mere form of speech for they were never allowed anywhere near it. When they neared the house they called out their own names loudly, so that the household was alerted to their defiled coming. Then Vishnudev's Father would come on to the porch of the house, take them to task for bellowing out like cattle, procure his ever present jug of holy water and sprinkle the surrounding air. Then wiping his ears (probably to expunge the sound of the shudras which had assaulted his sensitive Brahmin ears), he would proceed from the safe distance of the porch to bark out instructions for the day. Deja and his Father had never entered the gates which were separated from the house by a massive courtyard. Their journey ended at least five feet away from the gate, from where they shouted out to their benefactors. 'I've often wondered, you know,' Deja once told the boys, 'why people take offense at the shudra's habit of talking loudly. When the closest you are allowed to another person is fifteen feet or so, speaking softly is an indulgence we can ill afford.' The boys laughed at Deja's inherent sense of discrimination, his unexpected outbursts of muted temerity which momentarily struggled for dominance over the timidity in his eyes, though he would not dare to utter those words in front of anyone other than the boys.

'It must be some consolation to you Deja,' Birju told him, 'that the distance compels them to descend from their high caste perch and shout back at you.' And Deja threw his head back and laughed out loud, for the thought of a Brahmin behaving like a low caste had honestly never occurred to him. But swiftly, the deep irrational fear of his clan returned. 'Birju baba, you must not utter such words lest anyone hears you. You belong to the higher castes. It is your good fortune. Do not make the Gods angry by desecrating your status.' Even though he did not word his distress, the boys knew what he meant. He was afraid that any violation of the rigid caste lines would condemn Birju to a lower birth in his next life. Much as Deja's life was difficult and made more so by the upper castes, the boys knew he would never wish such a life for another. Deja feared too, the wrath the boys would have to face, if their people found out how frequently and freely they mingled with him.

Some days if they were lucky, after a hard day's work Deja and his Father would find Vishnudev's family's leftovers placed on a plate of dried leaves, a good distance from the gate of the house. If they were lucky. Often a stray dog would beat them to it. As a child Deja had asked his Father how as Harijans they could gather wood for Brahmins. His Father had scratched his head and confessed his ignorance. Back in their hamlet, the wisest man (wisest, Deja believed by virtue of being old and toothless) had said that fire is the supreme purifier. Since most of the wood was to be used as cooking fires, the Brahmins escaped defilement. A further question from Deja as to how the Brahmins carried the wood that the Harijans collected and deposited at the gates, into the house without suffering contamination, educed a sharp knock on his head and the acerbic comment that since he wasn't a Brahmin, in this birth at least, he needn't bear the burden of taxing his intellect.

When Deja was still a boy, Vishnudev married and had two beautiful children. A boy and a girl. The daughter had been married off at a young age and Deja recollected the grandeur of the ceremony, or at least those parts which his community had had the privilege of witnessing. He hadn't actually seen the bride of course, but he along with a few others of his hamlet had watched dumbstruck from a distance, as the bedecked ladies and the dapper men arrived for the nuptials. And the children! What a joy they were to behold. Never had he seen children attired the way they had been that day. And the spread the Harijans had enjoyed two days later! Leftovers no doubt, but a feast nonetheless. Vishnudev's son had studied in the city and after marriage had settled down there. Vishnudev lived alone in the huge house now, his wife having passed away four years after his son's marriage.

It was soon after that that life took a drastic turn for Deja. He was on his way back home after a day of back breaking work. Vishnudev now old and portly, but still blessed with remarkably vigorous vocal chords that roared out instructions, had directed Deja to cut out the weeds that had cropped up on his three-acre land. The sun had been merciless and Deja only had a mug full of water and a dry roti with onions that he had carried from home that day. It was when he was passing in front of the gates of Vishnudev's house that he heard the sound. A muffled cry, but easily identifiable as a call for help. Deja stood stock still, trying to figure out the direction the sound came from. Once more he heard the sound and in response shouted out his own name. 'Here… inside the gates man,' the voice called. 'Walk in, you – you goddamn fool.' For a moment Deja thought it was some demon trying to get him into trouble. Walk into the gates! He might as well walk onto his funeral pyre. 'It's me. Deja,' he shouted back. 'I cannot walk into the gates of this house.' He inched closer to the gates however, trying to target the source of the voice. 'Why don't you call the master?'

'I *am* the master, you fool!' Vishnudev's voice was now identifiable. 'Come quick, before…before you're doomed for having killed a Brahmin.'

Fear struck Deja's bosom at the words. Kill a Brahmin? What had he got himself into now? Being a pragmatic member of the lower caste, albeit a thwarted one, other thoughts crowded his mind. Kill a Brahmin? How does one do it from a distance of fifteen feet? Unless he practiced black magic? Was this a punishment for some transgression on his part? As he tried to sort out his thoughts, the voice came once again, strained now almost choking as if someone were throttling the life out of it. 'Deja, for God's sake man, walk into the gates and… come close…to…to the new well.' The voice faltered as if short of breath. 'I've fallen in…I can't hang on anymore. If I die you will be hounded for murd – murdering me and then you'll rot in hell for eternity.'

Deja could not believe his ears. Vishnudev was asking *him,* an untouchable for help. He could feel his body begin to tremble at the mere thought of walking into the gates, let alone helping Vishnudev. With folded hands, stooping shoulders and timid steps he approached the gates and shouted out. 'I'll get someone from the village to help you. I'll be massacred for coming anywhere close to you. I'll run and fetch the men.'

'You'll do no such thing,' Vishnudev called. 'I'll…I'll be a corpse by then and, and…and,' he gasped, 'they'll hang you for it. Get in, man. I'm your benefactor, am I not? I promise…I'll look after your family for the next ten generations Deja, just walk in and…and help me get upright.'

'You know,' Deja told the boys, 'even though he had one foot in the grave he was cutting a very shrewd deal, considering it was common knowledge that I had made up my mind to stay unmarried. Ten generations!'

The boys laughed and Hari put into words the question on everyone's mind. 'Why did you decide to stay unmarried, Deja?'

And once again his matter-of-fact and rational approach to life took them by surprise. 'Why me? I wish every untouchable would make a conscious decision not to get married. That way we don't have progeny and we save future generations from the ignominy of an untouchable's life.'

Having been half threatened and half cajoled Deja walked fearfully into the gates of Vishnudev's house. To his eyes the courtyard appeared huge, but he soon saw where the earth had been dug for a new well. A thick rope wound around four sticks dug into the ground at four corners isolated the dug up area. At one place the rope had moved into the hole in the ground as if dragged by some heavy weight and the four sticks bent towards the hole with the pull. 'Deja, have you gone?' Vishnudev's voice was muffled now. 'No master,' he replied. 'I am here. What am I to do?'

'Come close to the well, Deja. My foot is stuck, entangled in …the ropes.'

Deja went close to the well and peered down the sides. It was all he could do to keep from laughing. Vishnudev, the proud and virtuous Brahmin was hanging upside down in the half dug well. He had probably slipped while walking near it and his left foot was caught in the rope that ringed the freshly dug well to demarcate it and warn onlookers, while his right foot kept jerking to find a strong foothold. His portly frame was inverted (no doubt, appealing to gravity), and his hands tried in vain to clutch at something tangible and solid in the soft mud wall. When he spoke he had to move his face sideways and get the mud out of his mouth before he tried to speak and he gasped with the effort. 'Not surprising,' Deja had thought. 'Those arms can't be expected to cope with a load those legs can barely manage.'

'What are you staring at Deja? Do…something,' he gasped again. 'No, no. My hands first. If you free my foot I'll…I'll just fall in. Careful now, careful.'

The unfinished well had been dug about ten feet deep. Deja now galvanized into action, found a length of a long stout branch and thrust it into the depths of the well. In the soft but thick muddy water he first made sure it had a firm grip, then, guided it towards Vishnudev's hands. 'Grab it, master. And hold it while I carve out a foothold for you.' It was a sight to behold. The master upside down on the side of the well, now resting his hands on the tip of the branch that stayed rock solid buried in the shallow depths of the well. Intermittently his free foot flailed and he steadied himself like a gymnast, pressing the foot against the side of the wall while Deja worked away at the edge of the well. Slowly, with one hand grabbing hold of the left foot and the other working tediously at the rope that had tightened its grip on the Brahmin's flesh, Deja worked away for the better part of what seemed to him like an era. The fact that Vishnudev's weight was at least twice that of the man trying to free him, didn't help. Deja tried several uncomfortable positions before successfully maneuvering the imprisoned foot to freedom.

'Don't let go my…my…my foot, Deja,' Vishnudev wheezed. 'Or else I'll tumble into the well. I'm not…not very good at balancing this branch. Do be quick Deja…be quick.'

'Only a moment master and then I'll be done.' He freed Vishnudev's foot from its trap and holding on tight, lay face down on the ground and inched his free arm slowly down the side of the wall. 'Raise your right leg, master.' The leg moved of its own volition. 'No, no master not to the side. Put your foot down…I mean up. Up, so that I can grab it. Right, once more master. Up…up – aha.' At last, he had both of Vishnudev's ankles in his hands. How absurd they must have looked. Vishnudev, face down on the side of the well, with his hands resting on a broken branch entrenched in the water, his legs straight up in the air, ankles held by Deja who lay flat on the ground. 'Now I'll pull you up, master.'

'Slowly, Deja…slowly. Oh my poor…heart, it'll…burst…any moment. Slowly, slowly.'

Not that the injunction was necessary. With the kind of weight at his disposal Deja's pace could only be gradual. Finally, after what felt like an age to both men, Vishnudev was out of the well. He lay belly down on the ground, legs and arms spread-eagled, face turned sideways taking in mouthfuls of air and poor Deja on his knees, still clutching his master's feet trying to get back his breath.

That was the way three shocked villagers had found them. That was the moment Deja's life changed. Forever.

It was the biggest scandal of Ichhapurti. The very fact that Deja had entered the gates of a Brahmin house would have ensured his decimation. But three eyewitnesses had seen him actually in touch with the feet of Vishnudev, Ichhapurti's most revered Brahmin. It was a different matter that the reverence for Vishnudev was a derivative of a most un-Brahmin like factor, at least, one that the highest caste was given to repeatedly denouncing as being of no real value. For Vishnudev was the most fortunate of human beings. Not only was he a pure Brahmin, his family was one of the richest in the village.

In a village like Ichhapurti, it was a lethal combination, guaranteeing immediate if not permanent veneration.

Vishnudev himself had acted admirably. 'In the sense,' Deja said, 'that his acting skills were worthy of admiration. He swiftly regained his composure – I realized later – at the cost of his memory. He said the last thing he remembered was that he had been walking near the well to inspect how far the work had progressed and the next thing he knew he felt a push and had gone head first, down the side of the well.'

The boys cried out their indignation at the lie. 'But couldn't they see for themselves, Deja?' Birju demanded. 'Did they not look into the ditch and see the branch you'd stubbed into the ground to help the old devil? Did you do nothing to defend yourself?'

'Baba, what could I have done? The closest I had ever come before this to people outside my caste was thirty feet. And Vishnudev repeated the story of me being possessed by a demon so determinedly, that even I began having doubts as to my sanity at the time. Being among those people, I really couldn't get myself to believe I had had the gumption to walk into the gates of my master's house. Back then it seemed like I was facing all the fury of the Gods. I did realize after all, that I had committed a big sin.'

'Shut up, Deja,' Birju intervened. 'There is no such thing. One God created us all, didn't he? Then having one Father makes us equal. Why didn't you speak the truth?'

'I tried, but it isn't easy to speak when ten people sprinkle the surroundings with holy water and chant a blessed mantra every time I open my mouth to say something. And how could I defy a Brahmin's word? It is easy to argue in favor of the underdog, as long as he is someone else. It dawned on me then, that the incessant chanting was a blessing in disguise. If ever I had succeeded in making myself heard, I would have been stoned to death on the spot for opposing the word of a Brahmin.'

Even in his turmoil Deja was generous to the architect of his present condition. 'I could have been killed, you know, but my master told them that I must have been possessed by the devil at the time, or else I wouldn't have dreamt of doing such a thing. In fact, after I'd been condemned to roam the unholy woods in solitary confinement, he reiterated his promise to look after ten generations of mine.'

He smiled meekly at his attempt at humor.

The boys looked from Deja to each other. Though he said it in a soft murmur, they felt the pain that Deja must have gone through. Having risked his life to save a Brahmin he had been excommunicated not only from the main lanes of the village but from his own community as well. His parents had died when he was in his teens. His own friends and relatives would have nothing to do with him, for in their eyes he had fallen. So ingrained in the untouchables' psyche was the sense of inferiority that the mere thought of trying to break out of the mold brought on rushes of fear and anger. And Deja had not even ventured anything of the kind. He had merely tried to save Vishnudev. And to the untouchables in his hamlet that was unforgivable. Because of him, the others in the hamlet would run the risk of not being trusted even with the menial jobs they were now doing. One must not forget where one comes from, was a frequent exhortation in his hamlet. To make things worse, most of them believed Vishnudev's version of the story. In Deja's hamlet, in the one place his story was allowed to be told and heard, he had not been believed.

Vishnudev on the other hand, had come out of the episode in flying colors. People lauded him for his merciful attitude towards someone who had tried to kill him. Empathy, truthfulness, mercy even for his would be murderer, piety, all seemed to come gushing forth from his persona. He was hailed as the picture of a perfect Brahmin.

It was a picture that unfailingly sent Birju into a fit of rage. And Deja, as always, tried to calm him. 'What does it matter, Birju baba? It is not as if I was living the life of a king before this happened. I didn't lose much, except maybe a sense of belonging to my community.' He paused for a moment before going on. 'But ties that are wrecked so effortlessly are best broken. And look at the bright side. Nobody gives me any work, so I don't have to do any work at all. And my master provides food for me once a day.'

'He does that only to assuage his guilt and enhance his image, Deja. And what does he feed you? Two dried rotis and his spoonful of leftovers? Don't be fooled into thinking that the devil is your supporter.'

'I know, baba. But if through me he believes he can wash himself of some guilt then so be it. Why must I grudge him his share of penance?'

It was in moments like this one that the boys wondered if Deja was really what he pretended to be. He had almost no sense of self and the one person who had ruined his life, could stir up in him little more than undeserved consideration and pity. To Birju especially it brought a deep sense of shame and anger. Shame, that his community could so brazenly destroy another life. Anger, that the whole village could stand back and let it pass without a murmur of protest. Anger too that someone who was so obviously an intelligent, thinking human being could be so readily converted to a sense of his own unworthiness.

Sometimes Birju felt like grabbing Deja by his shoulders and yelling at him to wake up and take his life into his own hands. Why did he let a handful of goons dictate his life to him? Why didn't he gather the courage to put up a fight? Why didn't he go away somewhere and start life afresh? This last question he put to him. Deja looked at the boys and then his gaze moved away, a faraway look creeping into his eyes as if he was looking deep into the past.

'Birju baba, I was born in Ichhapurti. Even though my community disowns me now, I am bound by a sense of belonging to the place that I grew up in. The moment I step out of Ichhapurti, I am like the lost wandering ghosts of those dead whose unfulfilled desires not only bind them to this earth but bar the other worlds to them.' He paused for a moment and the faraway look rested on the three boys. 'Out there I will not only be an untouchable, I will also be a nobody. Here, at least I am the madman of Ichhapurti.'

It was then, at that moment, that it dawned on Birju's young mind how vital a sense of belonging is to man.

Hari-jan. Birju whispered the sound slowly in his mind. Years ago Mahatma Gandhi had coined the word to describe India's untouchables. Harijan. People of God: though in later years, they refused to answer to that moniker. Birju thought he understood now. Even being an untouchable is an identity; for many, the only one. And the fact that his people refused to recognize him as one of their own had brought greater sorrow to Deja than the unjust retribution he endured for an offense he had not committed.

Deja took his first troubled steps out of the woods about six months after he was exiled. His faithful friend, Bittu, had not shown himself the past three days. He had waited last night, the third night without Bittu and in the morning when he hadn't turned up Deja decided he had to do something about it. Bittu was his constant companion and his absence was a big blow to Deja, who had begun treating him like his child. He would talk to Bittu and recount his days as a child, his parents, and the games he played with his friends. Often, he told Bittu how lucky he was to be a dog. And how blessed he himself was to have Bittu for a companion. Bittu would lie contentedly next to Deja and for all purposes seemed to take in everything that his friend told him. Sometimes when he sensed that Deja was miserable, he would rest his face on Deja's knee and gaze lovingly into the lonely man's eyes. To Deja, who had scarcely ever encountered anything even close to real love and devotion, they were the most beautiful eyes in the world. He would smile at Bittu and gently stroke his head with his bony fingers. He longed to see him again, for he missed his companionship. The woods were not the same without him. It would be four more days before the boys would come to visit him and he had taken the decision to go and look for the dog himself. After all, he only had to keep away from the main streets of Ichhapurti. He had no desire to see the village or its inhabitants for he feared their reaction on seeing him. But he couldn't get Bittu out of his head. What if he was lying somewhere, injured and unable to fend for himself? Or maybe the villagers had killed him knowing he spent his days and nights with Deja. The uncertainty was more than Deja could bear. If only he gathered the courage to go to the village he might get news of Bittu. Good news or bad, at least it would end his uncertainty.

He stood for what seemed to him like ages, at the edge of the woods. His feet, apparently with a mind of their own, refused to budge from their chosen spot, even though he knew he would have to risk entering the village if he wanted to find out anything about Bittu. Then with some effort he willed his feet to move and found himself moving rapidly towards his destination. To Deja, it felt as if any slackening of his pace would serve as reason enough to cut short his perilous journey and return to the safety of the woods. Within minutes he was in sight of the outer street of the village. He did not stop till he came on to the dusty strip of road and then came to a halt most abruptly. The mere sight of this road that he had walked on as a free man for so many years filled his heart with a sense of bereavement. It wasn't only his sense of self that the villagers and his own community had snatched away from him. They had destroyed a man's instinctive desire to live in the past, when the present is made unbearable. They had destroyed the basic urge for refuge that a man seeks in the light of happy memories that cast their hopeful glow on the dawn of a better future. Deja had steadfastly refused to dwell in his memories, for he dared not hope for anything. Looking back would only mean mourning the loss of happier days, for nothing could persuade him to the vision of a better future. Now as he stood on the threshold of his village frontier, the sight and the very air seemed to drive into him a renewed sense of loss, of all those intangible gifts which, when life is as yet unfettered, man never suspects himself to be in possession of. For some reason that his troubled mind was unable to fathom, his heart was filled with an aching sense of grief and tears gathered in his eyes. He breathed slowly and deeply of the morning air as if the very act of breathing was something he was only just discovering. Now that he was here he realized just how much he missed his former life. The mere sight of the village had brought home to him his longing to be back as a normal inhabitant, to be one of the many who roamed free in the streets of the village. He had tried, successfully perhaps, to keep out any thoughts of his unshackled days because they only served to dishearten him. Now in hindsight, having experienced isolation and desertion, the relatively free life of an untouchable seemed like a royal existence.

He closed his mind to the stream of unhappy thoughts and put an unsteady foot forward. Tentatively he placed it on the dirt road and rested it, then followed with his other foot. He stood like that for a long time, fists clenched, his slender frame trembling at the sight of his beloved village.

Just a few yards to his left a well beaten path made its way to Deja's erstwhile hamlet.

He looked at the dirt road he had walked on for the better part of his life and then, as a sudden onrush of emotion engulfed him, Deja went down on his haunches, covered his face with his hands and wept. It was the first time since his exile that he cried.

He sat like this for a long time, till he was aware of a subdued buzzing sound. He raised his tear stained face to see a motley crowd of onlookers. Familiar faces looked down on Deja and unbeknownst to him a smile lit up his face. How wonderful it was to behold a known face.

'He smiles, actually smiles,' a vicious voice broke the spell. 'Only a shudra can survive his sense of humiliation.'

'What do you expect, brother? After all he can't help being a shudra, and we can hardly blame a madman.' And the crowd broke out into raucous laughter.

And Deja remained rooted to the spot, rudely jolted into his senses by the mocking voices. He sat staring at nothing in particular. A few minutes ago he had been unable to put a foot on Ichhapurti's soil. Now, even being made a target for derision and ridicule could not prevent him from staying his ground. He would leave only when he got news of Bittu, not before. He scanned the crowd for a face that was not unkind and at last settled on old Biren Das, who by virtue of being a non-Brahmin seemed a safer person to address. He was also someone Deja knew to be kind at heart, for he had seen him treat his servants with as much dignity as his status allowed, without adversely affecting his merit as a member of a distinguished upper caste.

'Sahib,' Deja, still squatting, pleaded with folded hands. 'I have only come to seek my dog, Bittu. I haven't seen him for three days and three nights. I fear the worst for him. If anyone can tell me where he is, or even that he is in good fettle, I shall go away instantly.'

Biren Das opened his mouth to speak to Deja, but sensing the eyes of the crowd on him he changed track and beckoned to his servant, who accompanied him on his morning walks to the river banks.

'Have you heard anything of the shudra's dog?'

'I have only just understood that he has a dog, master,' the servant replied.

'Then tell him that we have nothing to say.'

The servant looked from his master to Deja and began to utter a few words but was interrupted by a commotion at the end of the street. The crowd turned to look at the source of the noise and a gasp of surprise emanated from the group.

For the very pious Vishnudev was in the process of sanctifying the back streets of Ichhapurti with his presence. Never before in living memory had a high ranking Brahmin ever deigned to set foot on the back streets of the village. A passing servant, on seeing Deja, had run all the way to Vishnudev's house to warn him that his would-be assassin had dared to return. Vishnudev had not wasted a moment and here he was now, walking purposefully towards the crowd, with his ever present jug of holy water. The crowd reverently parted to let him through. Already, there were voices praising Vishnudev for his gallantry. He had come down to these streets to face his alleged murderer. A glorious Brahmin, from whom surely even great Kshatriyas themselves could take lessons on bravery and courage.

'What is this madman doing here?' Vishnudev's eyes were trained on Deja but his words were addressed to the crowd. Deja, still squatting with folded hands, looked up at Vishnudev.

Biren Das' servant moved forward. 'Swamiji, he says he has come looking for his dog.'

'The pariah has a dog? Has anyone seen this dog before?'

The crowd raised a murmur of denial.

'Tell him he must not look for pretexts to enter the village. The elders were kind enough to bar him only from Ichhapurti's main streets, but let him not undertake to exploit their merciful hearts.'

The servant repeated Vishnudev's words for Deja's benefit and then to the crowd's immense surprise, Deja spoke.

'I have only come to seek my dog. I wish for nothing else. If I will just get news that he is alright I shall go away, I seek nothing for myself.'

Vishnudev almost exploded in anger. 'In six months of exile the shudra has acquired nothing but the audacity of speech in my presence. This will not do. I must speak with him alone.'

The crowd set up an uproar. What! Vishnudev to be left alone with the madman? With his would-be assassin? Surely, there are limits even to courage and daring. But Vishnudev was Vishnudev. The street was cleared and Vishnudev was left alone with Deja. Not alone in actual fact. For people crowded the far end of the street and the narrow by-lanes, craning their heads and their necks, jostling intervening shoulders and arms to bear witness to Ichhapurti's second most exciting day in six months.

They watched as Vishnudev stood erect, with his hands locked behind his back and Deja looked up at him. They were two very different Vishnudevs. To the man in the crowd, the erect back and locked hands were redolent with supreme confidence and nerve. If the same man were to glance at Vishnudev's face, he would have been astounded at the extent of deviation in his demeanor. There was no confidence and nerve here, only a man of nervous disposition. For, Deja's arrival had signaled the advent of difficult days for the wily Brahmin.

Vishnudev closed his eyes, then, slowly opening them, turned his head to make sure that no one was within earshot. His bulbous eyes scanned the street and then satisfied that no one could hear him he turned to Deja.

'What on earth have you come here for? Speak the truth now.'

'Master, I only seek to take my dog back with me. He has been a faithful companion since the day of my exile and I haven't seen him for three days in a row.'

Vishnudev's eyes narrowed. 'You are not lying to me, are you? You haven't come here with the idea of deceiving people with some new yarn about me having called out to you for help, have you?'

'Master!' A look of alarm passed over Deja's face. 'I would not dream of it. Was I not possessed that day? You said so yourself. And anyway, who in his right mind would heed me?'

Vishnudev glared at the man in front of him. 'You are not the only one not in his right mind. Many in Ichhapurti itself can lay claim to that distinction. It is not a question of the truth here. If you repeat a thing often enough, a fair number of fools can be coaxed into believing anything.'

'But master, I have only come for my dog. I swear on all that is holy.'

'It had better be so. If ever it comes to my ears that you have been trying to abuse my goodwill, your fate will be sealed. I do not wish to see you ever again……'

'But master,' Deja pleaded. 'I cannot go without my dog, or news of him.'

Vishnudev turned back once more to see the crowd slowly almost hypnotically heaving its way towards them. He waved an imperious hand and the crowd moved back as one beast.

Tapping one foot on the ground, he turned to Deja. 'What kind of a dog is it?'

Deja thought for a moment. How was one to distinguish a dog?

He put the question to Vishnudev.

'You fool!' the old Brahmin spat out. 'I do not have all the time in the world to spend talking to a shudra. What color was he? Thin, fat, tailed, tailless…?'

'The color of muddied water, master. A tail that is never at rest, and lean, master. Lean, as I am, after all he is my dog.'

'I shall see what I can do. Now go back and stay away from here.'

But Deja was unusually dogged and resolute.

'Master, I will go as soon as I get my dog or…'

'Or news of him,' an exasperated Vishnudev cried.

Vishnudev knew better than to push his luck. He had seen people who had lost all sense of self, willing to risk their lives for a higher cause. The man who failed to see meaning in his own life, was perfectly capable of laying it down for an outside cause he perceived as noble. In fact, Vishnudev's own life experience had convinced him that the man who had nothing to lose, was the only man to be feared.

'Not only does this madman have nothing to lose,' Vishnudev deliberated, 'he poses the additional hazard of being a shudra. Can't count on him being predictable. I've got to do all I can to humor him or else he might start talking, and that's exactly what the Prasad brothers want.'

Vishnudev knew he had to tread cautiously.

'What will you do till then?' he asked Deja.

'I shall wait here till I get news of him.'

'Okay,' Vishnudev answered. 'As soon as you get news of him though, you must go away.'

'I promise to do so, master.'

Vishnudev turned back once more to see the familiar forward surge of the crowd and he spoke quickly.

'I will send people to look for your dog. Meanwhile you will say nothing of – .'

'I will not open my mouth, master.'

'Good,' the old man said and turned back abruptly to enlighten the expectant crowd.

The news sped as fast as the wind and the whole of Ichhapurti was agog in anticipation.

Even now, in his old age, Vishnudev had not lost his mettle. What glory he would bring to Ichhapurti! To forgive your would-be assassin was one thing, but he had actually gone and faced him. Unaccompanied, no less! And now he was galvanizing people to look for Deja's dog because it was the shudra's only companion. How compassionate and humane was his outlook! Surely Ichhapurti's soil was blessed to have one like Vishnudev walk its ground. And the villagers paid tribute to Vishnudev for exalting the back streets of Ichhapurti with his presence.

That the backstreet escaped elevation to a place of pilgrimage, following its supposed consecration, was nothing short of a miracle.

And so, under Vishnudev's resolute directions, a handful of the lesser mortals of Ichhapurti embarked on a hunt for Deja's dog. It was a sight to behold. In villages like Ichhapurti the untouchable as an individual, is indistinguishable, because for the others, differentiating one shudra from another is a pointless exercise. One shudra is very like another. It is no different with the village dog.

In India's villages the dog, like the shudra, is barred from homes. He may keep guard and bark at intruders. Indeed, that much is expected of him, but he must do so from a distance; though in case of the dogs the villagers are less rigorous in enforcing the rule of distance. The dog shares one more attribute with the shudra. Like him, one dog is very much like another.

And so it was that a strange sight met visitors to Ichhapurti that day. It seemed as if all the men and boys of Ichhapurti were in quest of a dog. Within four hours the air was resonant with the feral noise of barking. Not one or two but twenty of them had been caught and shackled, ready for display. Vishnudev hiding behind the opportune taxonomy of 'Brahmin', the fact that he absolutely dreaded dogs, stayed away from the scene. He hated dogs and most of the village lads were sure of the dogs returning the honor.

On his instructions, the vociferous creatures were taken to where Deja still waited in unwearied anticipation.

From a distance of thirty feet, Deja closely inspected the dogs. But Bittu was not among them. If he had been there, he would have bridged the gap in an instant. The entire village turned up to watch Deja scrutinize the pack and with every dog that was paraded, the congregation held its combined breath. But with every rejection, the crowd got uneasy and soon news reached Vishnudev's anxious ears that Bittu, the dog, was not among the brood.

For one panic stricken moment, Vishnudev feared that the shudra was out to make a fool of him. After all, he had managed to get the entire village to assemble at one place.

In fact, he had got Vishnudev to do it for him! If the wretched animal remained elusive, Vishnudev could count on the shudra being a regular visitor to the village. His frequent arrival in the village would only ensure the prospect of his appearance being treated with tolerance. If he was allowed to walk regularly into the village, it wouldn't be long before he loosened his goddamn mouth to receptive ears. For all the vociferous adulation showered on him, Vishnudev was in no doubt that more than one man in Ichhapurti was more than willing to stick a knife into him. Vishnudev was also a man of considerable foresight. He knew the village would oblige him for a few days with the canine pageant. Beyond that, when the novelty wore off they would forget the shudra, but he, Vishnudev, would find the spotlight of ridicule trained on him. Man is an unreliable animal, after all. He knew just how effortlessly the people of Ichhapurti could mutate their blatant approval of him to covert contempt. That was one thing he must never risk. There had to be a way out. He couldn't allow the obnoxious shudra to gain a foothold in Ichhapurti once again.

Deja stayed rooted to the spot all day, going back to the woods only when the shadows began their drive against the light. He trudged slowly homeward to the woods, his shoulders drooping from weariness and hunger. Tonight, he would go to sleep hungry. For Deja it was nothing new. He had for so long endured a partial satiation of the appetite that a day or two of hunger was easy to stomach. He worried about Bittu, but was glad that his journey to the village had not gone unnoticed by his three friends. He had seen them watching, a little away from the crowd. Now that they knew about Bittu, he was sure they too would be on the lookout for him. Never mind, he would try again tomorrow.

Vishnudev was in a real dilemma now. He desperately wanted, with all his heart, to keep Deja out of sight and out of mind. As of now he couldn't persuade the man to keep away of his own accord. Forcing him to stay away might turn out to be counterproductive. He had to tread carefully now. Not only did he have to prevent Deja from becoming a frequent visitor to the village, he had to uphold the elevation of his reputation since the shudra incident. The villagers held him in increasingly high regard for the way he had conducted himself. At least, for the way that they perceived he had conducted himself. He could never let that dwindle, for it would signal the death of Vishnudev's dominance in the very lucrative Brahmin way of life. If the men of the village sensed that his word could no longer keep Deja away from the village, that his orders were ignored by a mere shudra, he might as well wave goodbye to performing the villagers' traditional ceremonial rituals. It would mean an end to his stature as Ichhapurti's most revered Brahmin. In fact, an end to a very generous source of income. The vision of the Prasad brothers and other vultures that he suspected of waiting in the wings, taking over a substantial part of his business (for that is what it was), kept him awake at night. It wasn't the money. He had enough of that and some more. It was that indefinable something. That intangible spin-off, that made people bow their heads in reverence and sycophantic deference. He wasn't just a Brahmin. He was a moneyed Brahmin and that was what had allowed him to keep his hold on the villagers. The men in the village could easily discount a Brahmin.

It is relatively easy to disregard a purely spiritual man. But Vishnudev was no ordinary Brahmin. The compelling forces of native Brahmin superiority and obvious affluence that came together in Vishnudev, had guaranteed him an unwavering client list. He didn't mind losing the money, but he dreaded the thought of losing their respect. Without their reverence, the esteem they held him in, even though he knew them to be insincere and hollow, Vishnudev was as good as dead. By himself, without an approving audience, Vishnudev was nothing.

So it was that the night of Deja's reappearance in the village, Vishnudev called a meeting of the villagers. The more eminent members sat on chairs placed under the banyan tree in the village grounds and discussed the burning topic of the day. The others lounged about wondering what matter commanded their urgent attendance. Surely Deja hadn't managed to assemble them at one place for a second time in one day?

When the illustrious group concluded their hushed discourse, Devi Prasad raised a hand and silence ensued.

'My dear brothers,' Birju's Father began. 'As you are all probably aware, the shudra we had collectively barred from our village paid us a visit today. It is his good fortune that our honorable Vishnudev takes a lenient view of his transgression. I for one, am sure no one else in Ichhapurti has the courage or the desire to do the same.' He turned sideways to look at Vishnudev and folded his hands in a reverent gesture. Facing the crowd once again, Devi Prasad continued. 'It was the conclusion of not one, but each one of us, that the shudra must be banished with immediate effect from the limits of Ichhapurti. But Vishnudev, in his wisdom and more so, in his inexhaustible compassion has refused to lend his endorsement to the decision. It is his opinion that a solitary life in the woods has probably unhinged the shudra and that we must humor him, if only for a few days. If he says he had a dog for company – we must concur.'

A disgruntled murmur did its rounds at the words. Humor a shudra? A mad shudra?

And the villagers were expected to accommodate *him*? A man of keen observation would have noticed a barely perceptible smile flicker across Birju's Uncle, Vijay Prasad's face at the reaction of the crowd. If he was even more acute in his observation, the man would have noticed the smile relocate from Vijay Prasad's lips to settle down in his eyes, contemplating a very difficult future for his rival Vishnudev.

Devi Prasad raised a hand to silence the crowd, then looking at Vishnudev and receiving a nod of his head as sanction to keep going, turned to face the crowd once again.

'My fellow citizens, I know it is very difficult for us to understand, to grasp, why a person such as the shudra must rouse so much consideration in our revered Vishnudev. Suffice to say that he is the very fount of mercy. The shudra's forefathers have worked for Vishnudev's family for ages, so he feels it is his duty to do all he can for the shudra, in spite of his transgressions.'

The crowd nodded its head in general understanding. 'However,' Birju's Father continued, 'we cannot allow a situation to develop wherein the shudra thinks it is his normal right to walk onto the streets of the village.'

Again the gathering nodded its collective head in vigorous assent. Yes, yes they said to one another. He must never be allowed to think he's been pardoned.

'So we have arrived at a decision that has satisfied us and we are sure will not disappoint you either. It is dangerous, even foolish to ruffle the feathers of a madman, for one cannot say how he will react. And when the madman is a shudra, it is only wise to expect the worst. So, there is something, after all, in Vishnudev's approach towards the shudra.'

This time Vijay Prasad's smile was noticeable and he wasn't alone. Many in the crowd recognized the crafty albeit veiled affront on Vishnudev, who put on an indifferent mask while his insides squirmed within his ample form. The ambiguous accusation contained in the words gave Vishnudev just enough reason for offense but their subtlety deprived him of the required ammunition to vent his ire. If he protested, Devi Prasad would simply say he had not stated that Vishnudev feared the shudra, merely that a shudra in that situation is to be treated with a little consideration and Vishnudev's compassionate heart had providentially led him to the right decision. With a masterstroke, Devi Prasad had made the first dent in Vishnudev's holier-than-thou image. What a few in Ichhapurti had merely suspected, now several were convinced of. It was more than just his compassionate outlook that had prompted Vishnudev to take things lightly with the shudra. Fear, after all, can beget compassion in the unlikeliest of places.

'So it has been decided that we, the people of Ichhapurti, shall arrange one day of the week for the shudra to locate his dog. When he finally does track down his animal, he will be barred from Ichhapurti summarily. No backstreet concessions this time. If we have to keep him away we must find this dog of his and I ask all the men and boys of our village to join in this endeavor to keep our village unsoiled by the feet of ungrateful shudras.'

He paused to let the words sink in. There was still a hum of discontent doing the rounds. *This was way too much, to give in to a shudra. Why put up with him at all? What can he do anyway? But he was Vishnudev's man and he wished to accommodate him, if only for a few days. How long will he survive anyway? Who, Vishnudev? No, the shudra.*

The Prasad brothers were in a generous frame of mind. As far as they were concerned, Deja could visit Ichhapurti every single day. The more he came in contact with the villagers, the better. It wouldn't be long before someone's heart softened at the sight of the poor man and allowed him a few words now and then. And then it wouldn't be too long before willing ears sympathized with Deja's side of the story.

After a few minutes, all was quiet and Devi Prasad spoke at length about the virtues of sustained compassion and tolerance. At last, when he was sure he had spoken long enough to dampen any resistance in the crowd, he ended his speech.

'My friends, I think we must all concur on this decision. After all, this is for the good of our beloved village. If we work collectively, in a spirit of oneness we shall free our village forever from the evil shadow of this madman. And then, we must remember that compassion is the mark of a true human being. Let us not pass up this opportunity to demonstrate that Ichhapurti is a model village, that in spite of the inconvenience its people are ever ready to do that which is in the best interests of humankind.'

So the heads nodded again, not so much because they agreed with the Prasad brothers or with Vishnudev, but because it was late in the night by village standards and no one could be bothered enough to argue with the three men.

And so it was that every Sunday, Deja squatted at the same spot at the village boundary and studied the dogs. Soon people from nearby villages came to watch 'the madman of Ichhapurti' at work. The more enterprising ones brought dogs from their villages for him to inspect. Small boys laughed in joy when Deja, who kept thirty feet away even from the dogs, narrowed his eyes to start his examination of the creatures. Everyone found it hilarious when the dogs were forced to stand still and Deja moved a few feet here and a few feet there, always careful to maintain his approach limits to inspect them from all sides. Stray dogs in villages look practically like one another, unless they are lucky enough to wear a different color. All black dogs look alike, all brown dogs look alike and all spotted dogs look the same. Sometimes the same dog was repeatedly paraded in front of him and poor Deja would examine him in earnest all over again, much to the delight of the crowd. Deja would squat and call out to the dog. 'Bittu, my Bittu, is it you? Come to me, my friend. Come and we'll go home together.' And the crowd would laugh in glee at Deja's loving words, for in the villages, it had not crossed anyone's mind that animals, other than cattle which provided them with milk, could be the object of so much care and doting. Frequently, a dog would bark in response and strain at the leash, trying to get close to the man whose touch could only be more soothing than his voice. Given a chance, the dogs would have eagerly substituted for Bittu.

The boys tried to dissuade Deja from making an appearance. 'They come only to mock you, Deja.' Birju, was brutally honest as ever.

'How does it matter to me, why they come? They bring the dogs with them; that is all I am aware of. The more dogs they bring, the more likely I am to find Bittu.'

'But we've looked all over the village, Deja. He isn't here. Maybe he's gone off in one of the ferries across the river. You know the dogs do that.'

But Deja was not to be shaken off so easily. 'They bring dogs from across the river too, don't they? Maybe one day someone will get Bittu and then I can bring him back here with me.' A sad look passed over his features. 'People can be cruel to dogs, you know. I wish I knew where he is. If only I knew he was alright, I wouldn't worry so much.'

The three boys were struck dumb in amazement. People can be cruel to dogs, Deja had said! They had watched as an unkind world laughed, and mocked, and made fun of a man whose only failing was his abiding gentleness. Even after that, all they could get him to admit was people's cruelty to dogs.

Birju, as always, intended to set things straight.

'Deja, the world treats you cruelly too.'

'Maybe, Birju baba. But a dog is a dumb creature. It needs defending.'

'And you?'

'I can defend myself.'

'But you don't,' Hari protested.

'I have no need to, Hari baba. Defend myself against what? The laughter of a few people? Or the jibes of many? They are mere sounds, baba. Why fret over them?'

The three friends looked at each other and then at Deja. No sign of animosity marred his gentle features. He was as true as his word. Their time with Deja was full of surprises. Life itself was full of surprises for three boys only just beginning to test the waters of their adolescent years, only just beginning to grasp the immensity of the yawning divide between learning the truth and living it. But life's surprises on account of the elders who preached one word and acted to the contrary were ugly, inconsistent and unappealing. Time spent with Deja was full of surprises of the pleasant kind. He was an unlettered man, but in so far as the boys were concerned, Deja could have compiled a treatise on how to live life in the right spirit.

'Deja,' Birju said, taken aback by Deja's words. 'Deja, you ought to be a Brahmin, the way you talk.'

Instantly Deja was down on his haunches, folding his hands in front of him. 'Please, Birju baba. Do not, for God's sake, for *my* sake do not ever say such things. I am a shudra. Whatever happens to me will be an improvement. But I beg of you,' he said his eyes pleading, 'do not utter such words, they do not behove a Brahmin. You must not desecrate your holy status.'

And Birju promised not to repeat it ever again, because he saw that it truly distressed him. They stopped dissuading Deja from making his weekly appearance, for they realized that he was genuinely unmindful of both respect and ridicule.

Soon, Sundays turned into 'Madman of Ichhapurti days'. The sight became so popular and yielded so much economic dividend, that the villagers were no longer keen on barring Deja for life. Sundays meant money, for the boatmen who ferried people from the villages across the river, for tea stalls that kept the visitors refreshed with glasses of sweet tea, for the sweet shop owner and the balloon seller. For the man who sold peanuts, and wonderful cold ice cream, for the toy seller, the bangle seller, and the seller of buttermilk. Even the temple, whose precincts were barred to Deja and his community, found its coffers filling up thanks to the steady stream of visitors who came to watch Deja, but would not leave the village without paying their obeisance to the local deity. Deja was no ordinary untouchable now. He was a source of revenue, a fiscal miracle.

The shudras could no longer claim sole rights to unpredictability. The villagers had moved from not wanting to see Deja, to not being able to see enough of him. There was talk of getting Deja to come twice a week, but the idea was shot down as being uneconomical since most villagers were busy all week. And then, there was Vishnudev to contend with. Deja, twice weekly, might get too much for him.

Things had indeed turned into a nightmare for Vishnudev. Never in his dreams could he have foreseen the turn of events. Now even the villagers would oppose, although clandestinely, the very thought of barring Deja from the village. In Indian villages, a man in dire straits deems himself in urgent need – real or imagined – of a Brahmin as a gateway to God. A man doing fairly well for himself has no such compulsion. In this case at least, the urgent need was for the shudra.

It was nearly six months now, since the pageant of the dogs had begun and it showed no sign of abating. This would not do. Vishnudev's trusted servant who brought him all the village news, recounted how some of the villagers as well as some of the visitors had taken to speaking with Deja. Terror struck Vishnudev's heart at the very thought of it. If Deja grew in confidence, he might unburden himself to sympathetic ears. And sympathetic ears were often blessed with obliging tongues He could never permit that to happen.

There is an old saying in India which contends that, under certain circumstances man may be compelled to promote the jackass to the title of one's progenitor. Vishnudev had that in mind when he realized that however much he loathed the idea, it was time to strike a compromise with the Prasad brothers.

And so it was that Vishnudev found himself in the spacious Prasad home. The proceedings were not entirely unpleasant, with Vishnudev prudent enough not to ruffle any favorable feathers and the Prasad brothers keen to keep him in good spirits to draw the best out of an auspicious proposition.

It would have astonished Deja no end to be told that three of Ichhapurti's most respected men were discussing him late into the night. He would have been more than astonished if it were conveyed to him that the future prospects of the three men and what course it would take depended on him. More accurately, it depended on what happened to him. Deja would have been less than surprised to find out that they held his future in their hands.

Vijay Prasad was surprised to hear of Birju's jaunts in the unholy woods, but he took it in his stride. Bhola, his servant had spied the boys walking towards the unholy woods and out of curiosity had shadowed the three friends. He had been aghast at the sight that greeted him. Even though they maintained a distance from Deja, the very idea of the boys making their way to see him was scandalous. Bhola had run as fast as his faithful legs could carry him to his master, the revered village guru, Vijay Prasad. In thirty years of serving Vijay Prasad, Bhola had never seen him lose his calm at unfortunate news. Small everyday things that went wrong brought out the worst in him, like lunch delayed for a few minutes, or shoes that were not kept polished and readied at the threshold on his parting. Then, to observe him one would think the whole world had collapsed around the village guru. But bad news brought to him was usually with regard to someone else and that was easily digested. Bhola expected his master to explode in anger at the news of Birju and his friends, but was in for a surprise. Vijay Prasad merely enquired and confirmed if Bhola had witnessed the boys' trip with his own eyes and then cautioning him to take the news no further, dismissed him.

Unimpeded by the onus of parental liability, a bachelor is inclined to take a more tolerant view of juvenile insubordination. But Vijay Prasad also realized that if the report was true, which coming from Bhola it most certainly was, it wouldn't be long before Vishnudev found out about it through other sources. If he did find out, it would be the equivalent of holding a gun to the Prasad brothers' heads. Vijay Prasad was a man of quick decisions. He lost no time in informing his brother, Birju's Father Devi Prasad.

'That boy will be the death of me,' Devi Prasad said, running nervous fingers through his hair. 'Let him come home tonight, I'll teach him a lesson he'll never forget.'

'No, bhaiyya,' Vijay Prasad replied. 'We must think with a calm mind. Boys will be boys after all.'

'But this is serious, Vijay,' Devi Prasad replied. 'Imagine what would have happened if news of this had reached Vishnudev first.'

'I know, which is why I am saying we must tread carefully. You cannot antagonize boys of Birju's age, you know that. Things will only backfire. Forbid him from going there and you've practically guaranteed his visits to the shudra. No, we must think calmly.'

'What do you suggest, Vijay? My mind refuses to function.'

Vijay Prasad was silent for a long time. Devi Prasad looked at his younger brother and knew that he had already arrived at a solution. Vijay Prasad made decisions with the speed of lightning. And once he had made a decision his words would come slow and measured. Like the weekly satsang, the religious discourse he held for the people of Ichhapurti. He would hold the crowd spellbound with his knowledge and interpretation of the scriptures, his genius for weaving the threads of sacred wisdom seamlessly into the design of routine life. In villages like Ichhapurti, tabloids are easily dispensed with. Servants are a more dependable source of desired information, reliably accurate in their analysis and it was only fitting that the finest of men like Vijay Prasad retained the best informants. It helped make the satsangs more interesting and relevant. At the satsang, just before he wanted to nail home a point he was making, he'd fall into a kind of stupor. And then without warning his words would come with such crushing force and vitality that each one present would believe the words were addressed to him personally. And Bhola would congratulate himself on a job well done.

Devi Prasad waited. If Vijay Prasad was not perturbed, there was no reason to be. The next morning Birju was pleasantly surprised to be told by his Father that he was to take the ferry across the river to the big village with his friends to spend the day at the cinema, enjoy a picnic and spend the night at his cousin's place. Not surprisingly he was also uneasy. Why this sudden generous offer? What great event did they want Birju to escape? After all, the cinema was not a place his Father was likely to recommend. He went to his Mother, who he knew would not lie to him.

But Ma dissolved his doubts. 'You take your suspicions too far, Birju,' Ma said, 'when you question your own Father's motives. Just because we are past a certain age, growth is not denied us. Even today I am adapting to a changing world, maybe your Father is moving with the times too, maybe he really does want you to enjoy yourself.'

'With a little nudge from Vijay Uncle, no doubt,' Birju thought to himself. For all his hoary spiritual façade, Birju knew his Uncle to be contemporary in his outlook. He effortlessly merged the rigid black and white of spiritual diktats with the colorful abandon of modernity. When the older men complained of the allure of modern life that seemed to mesmerize the present generation, the village guru was inclined to take the side of the youth. 'One must not deride that which one has never experienced. Man is a creature of change. If man did not accept change and transformation, you would still till the land with your bare hands. Our children must learn from their own experiences.' Then he would shine a benevolent smile on his listener and say, 'Do not fear change. The thing to fear is fear itself.' And the man would exalt Vijay Prasad for his wisdom and go home wiser; at least in his own view. But even if the idea of the trip was Vijay Prasad's, he had to have a compelling reason for wanting to keep Birju away.

Hari and Kedar were surprised too. Kedar with his simplicity was inclined to take a positive view of the proceedings.

'Why must you always suspect people? If you keep on like this, we will never get anywhere at all. When we ask for permission to visit the cinema, it's mostly denied and when we *are* allowed you've got to spoil it with your perpetual questions.'

'But why all of a sudden, is what I'd like to know,' Birju insisted.

Hari was thoughtful. 'Why all three of us, is what I'd like to know? Father said I must go with you because your Father was keen for me to keep you company. The cinema is a welcome development, but I smell something cooking.'

'I'll tell you what,' Kedar said, excitedly. 'Go to your Father, Birju and tell him we do not wish to go tomorrow, but a week from today. If he's upset about it or insists we go tomorrow, then we know they want us out of the way for some reason. But if he agrees, then you must admit we're only exaggerating our misgivings.'

Hari and Birju looked in amazement at Kedar. Coming up with ideas was not his forte, but evidently he had taken the trouble to employ his brains today.

'You ought to be at the movies more often, Kedar,' Hari laughed. 'The mere mention of it has set your lazy brain to work.'

Kedar laughed good-naturedly. 'One must be good at something, sometime.'

Hari thought it was worth a try. It would be futile to ask pointed questions. Not only would he not receive a satisfactory answer, if they did have something in mind, it would only put them on their guard. And then miracles happened – it was entirely possible that his Father really did want to please his son.

So that evening Birju went to his Father who was sitting back contentedly on the divan conversing with his brother.

'Yes Birju?' his Father queried.

'I was wondering Father… if I can postpone the trip to the cinema to next week?'

'Why?' Birju's Father frowned.

'Why not?' Vijay Prasad cut in. 'You can go next week if you like, Birju, but go you must, lest your Father change his mind and you find yourself excluded from the delights of the cinema once again.'

'Yes, Uncle,' Birju replied and nodding his head at his Father who dismissed him with a wave of his hand, took leave.

So that was alright. If they had planned the trip only to get the boys out of the way, then surely Father and Uncle would have shown signs of agitation. Kedar had been right. He, Birju, was getting a little too suspicious for his own good. Birju was satisfied that there was nothing out of the ordinary, other than his imagination.

Back in the room, Devi Prasad glared at his younger brother. 'What on earth were you thinking of when you let Birju have his way just now? At the last minute, when everything's arranged!'

Vijay Prasad smiled at the angry face. 'Really, you don't know a thing about how to approach children. If we had insisted they go tomorrow, Birju would only get suspicious and that's the last thing we want, especially once the job's done. That boy of yours has brains *and* uses them. The whole village clings on to every word I say,' he said. 'But not our Birju. If there is any thinking to be done, you can be sure he'll do it on his own.'

'But everything's arranged, Vijay. We cannot let children dictate to us.'

'Sometimes it is in our interest to allow them that privilege,' Vijay Prasad answered. 'And what's arranged can easily be rearranged. After all, *we* are paying for the job. Don't worry, bhaiyya. I'll manage it.'

The boys went to see Deja one day before the trip was to materialize. Deja was as excited as the boys at the news. In fact, he couldn't have been more excited if he himself was to be going to the cinema.

'And keep your eyes open for my Bittu,' he said, when the boys got up to take leave.

The boys promised him they would and said goodbye. They walked away slowly, a nagging sense of guilt dragging at their feet. At the end of the dust road from where they always caught their last glimpse of Deja and waved goodbye to him, the boys stopped and looked back. For some reason, today, Deja appeared more alone than ever. He had always been a solitary figure. Even before his exile he was not inclined to too much speech, preferring to keep his own counsel. Though always ready with a smile, with Deja, words were difficult to come by. His parents had died when he was in his teens, he had few friends and he had chosen to stay unmarried, so he was used to his own company. But today, Deja looked lonely and desolate. He truly missed the dog he had lovingly tended to for more than five months and with each passing day a little bit of hope died in him. The boys knew he would have taken the first ferry that would agree to take him across the river to look for Bittu, had he been a free man. Maybe he wished he could go with the boys and look for Bittu himself. Each one of the boys felt the dismay in Deja's heart. Birju looked at the pathetic and dismal figure that stood gazing at them. To Birju it seemed like Deja was waving goodbye to his last hopes. He looked again at the thin, emaciated man with his hand still raised in silent adieu and for a moment Birju could feel his friend's undeserved unhappiness and loss, in his own soul. Something broke inside Birju's heart at the sight of the poor man and he raced back along the dust road towards Deja as fast as his nimble legs could carry him. No line on the ground could stop his momentum now and in a gesture that shocked both Deja and the boys, Birju just managed to stop himself in front of Deja, and taking both of Deja's shaking hands in his, looked at him through tear filled eyes. 'Don't worry, Deja,' he whispered to the startled man. 'We'll be back soon…maybe with Bittu. You're not alone Deja, we're your friends for life.'

Birju turned away before Deja could see the tears in his eyes burst their banks and trudged slowly back to his still startled friends.

Deja stood with folded hands, looking on as if in a dream at Birju's receding figure. By the time Birju reached his friends and walked away, Deja had buried his face in his hands and was weeping inconsolably.

Three very quiet friends made their way out of the unholy woods and on to the village road.

Kedar was disturbed at the turn of events. It was one thing to side with a shudra, but to go ahead and actually touch him…he wasn't so sure. He said so to his friends.

'Kedar, make up your mind. Either the shudras are as good as us or they are not. People like Deja have no need for your pity and sympathy. Equality is their right and it is what they truly desire. And deserve.'

'I know…but what I meant to say was that there is no need to get physical with them.' Kedar was back to his uncertain principles. 'Bathe with some holy water, Birju.'

'Oh shut up, Kedar.' Birju's anger was on the rise again. 'Get away from me if you want to borrow your forefathers' thinking habits.'

'Okay, okay,' Kedar backed off. 'Do what you want, but I do wish you'd go easy on the radical side of your personality. I'll see you at the satsang tonight.' Kedar had stated the rather unusual desire to attend Vijay Prasad's sermon that night in gratitude for the chance to watch a movie.

The boys met there and in keeping with their new found desire to express gratitude to Birju's Uncle, actually concentrated on his words. Soon the sermon came to a close.

'So, my brothers and sisters, remember that to feed a hungry creature is a virtuous act. God is in each one of us, in all His creations. Every time you feed a hungry mouth, human or otherwise, you repay a debt long overdue. Nothing is more pleasing to God than to be fed through the mouth of a poor hungry creature. Tonight on your way home from the satsang, remember my words when you see a stray dog. Remember my words when a hungry crow comes calling tomorrow at your kitchen window. Yes, my children, if you see a man feed and serve a helpless creature, bow to him for that is how God wishes you to be. God be with you tonight on your way home. Bless you all. Om.'

And folding his hands in a gesture of leave taking, Vijay Prasad closed the holy book in front of him, slowly stretched his rheumatic knees and gently straightened himself to his full stature. The people of Ichhapurti waited respectfully for him to move away from the seat under the banyan tree, where he delivered his weekly discourse on the holy books.

'Well, well,' Birju whispered to his friends. 'Looks like our obeisance to Deja is long overdue.'

'What do you mean?' Kedar queried.

'Didn't you hear my Uncle?' Birju answered. 'If you see a man feed and serve a helpless creature, bow to him. As far as I can see, Deja is the only one in Ichhapurti who refused to eat before he fed his dog.'

Hari giggled at Birju's words. 'Don't let anyone hear you, Birju. If they do your Father and Uncle will skin you alive.'

The boys parted ways at the main street and agreed to meet early next morning to catch the first ferry to the town across the river.

The boys took the best seats on the ferry. A trip on the ferry was exciting by itself, without the added attraction of the movies. Kedar laughed in delight at the sight of birds that swooped down into the water in pursuit of fish. Birju loved everything to do with water, even the sound of the boat cutting through the water as it made its way ashore. Only Hari had his doubts. On his way to the river this morning, he had seen Birju's house servant Bhola with two ruffians, whose services Hari knew were summoned only when violence was indispensable. Bhola had been flustered at the sight of Hari and had acted as if the two ruffians were merely crossing his path. He urged Hari on, saying he was late for the ferry. Hari knew otherwise. He had started with more than enough time on his hands because he had intended to watch the first boat that waved its way onto Ichhapurti's shores. There was something magical about watching the small triangular hull of the boat in the distance transform itself into the large ferry as it docked at Ichhapurti. He shrugged off the uneasy feeling and walked on towards the river. The sight of the boat shut out all misgivings and the ride in the ferry practically got rid of any lingering fears.

They watched the far shore get closer and more real as their boat approached the landing.

Their first stop was the local tea shop, where they tucked into soft sweet bread dotted with tutti-frutti and even sweeter glasses of tea. None of the boys were allowed tea at home and they soaked in the sense of independence and adulthood that came with its consumption. They moved on quickly to the movie theatre, a small rather ramshackle building which nevertheless drew enough people to keep it functioning. They bought tickets for the movie and Kedar was delighted that it was an action flick.

They laughed at the exaggerated antics of the comic in the movie, and stared in awe at the shots of beautiful faraway locales. It was a rerun of an old regional film, but the boys didn't mind. Kedar made the most of his time, even clapping wildly at what he considered to be exceptional fight sequences. After a thoroughly riotous hour and a half, the boys walked out of the theater into the noonday sun. Birju shielded his eyes with the curve of his elbow and located the small eatery opposite the theater that his Uncle Vijay Prasad had said was not to be missed at any cost. They crossed the small street and walked into the place where the air was saturated with the mingling of different aromas. Kedar nosed out samosas and dahi puris, and with eyes closed unerringly led them to a table laden with the sweet burden of jalebis and malpuas. Hari laughed as Birju and Kedar kept changing their minds about what to eat, as they inspected the enormous array of snacks and sweets.

They finally decided on their feast and sat down at a table.

'Hey, Birju!'

Birju turned around to see Lakhan. He had recently moved from Ichhapurti to this village with his family.

'What a surprise to see you here!' Lakhan sat down at their table. The three boys smiled at him. They remembered their days with this wild boy, who was ready for just about anything. In fact, it was one of the reasons his family had moved out of Ichhapurti, so that they could live near Lakhan's maternal Uncle, who was the only person who commanded his respect and obedience. Not surprising, considering that the Uncle in question was the reigning wrestling champion of the district.

'So? What brings you here?' Lakhan queried.

'We came to watch a movie, Lakhan. We watched the morning show.'

'You've come all the way from Ichhapurti to watch a movie? You lucky devils. And look at me…I stay here and I cannot even dream of entering the cinema halls.'

'What?' Kedar was shocked. 'What's stopping you?'

'WHO, Kedar; who's stopping me is the question.'

'Alright then, who?'

'The reigning wrestling champ, who else? Says he will break every limb of my body if he ever gets to hear that I've been to the movies.'

The boys stared in disbelief, then laughed at the comical look on Lakhan's face.

'Don't look so sad, boys,' Lakhan cheered them up. 'I do manage to sneak in now and then, you know.'

'I thought so,' Birju laughed. 'I don't think anyone can keep you from the things you've set your sights on.'

'Say, what's going on with the madman? Something's cooking, isn't it?'

'Don't call him that.' Birju's voice was cold.

Hari intervened. 'What do you mean something's cooking?' He felt his feet go cold at the words, as his morning encounter with Bhola came to mind.

'I don't know, really. You know my Uncle. People approach him to get their dirty work done. Saw a couple of Ichhapurti men a few days ago with him. They were saying something about handling the madman.'

'When?' Hari stood up as if yanked by an imaginary hook.

'Why, what's the matter?'

Birju and Kedar stared in amazement as Hari thundered at Lakhan.

'Can't you answer a simple question? When did you hear about it and what were they planning?'

'Look here, Hari. My Uncle doesn't let me in on his doings. I only found out because there was some ruckus last week and the men who were supposed to do the job were grumbling about wasted time. Said they had better things to do than being put on and then put off a job by a fool like Vijay Prasad.' He looked at Birju. 'Sorry about that, but that's what they said.'

'Go on,' Hari urged the lad.

'Nothing to go on about. They were upset because there was a last minute change in the timing of the job. I know two of my Uncle's men went over to Ichhapurti last night, so I thought something was… hey, what?'

Hari let out a cry and sped out of the eatery, motioning to Birju and Kedar who followed, leaving behind a very baffled Lakhan.

They ran towards the ferry that was just readying to leave for Ichhapurti. Three very quiet and fearful boys sat through the journey. Hari told them about seeing Bhola in the morning with the two ruffians. No one laughed at the clever birds that dove into the water; neither did anyone hear the soothing sounds of the wake. There was nothing beautiful about the shining sun. But each one looked out restlessly to the shores of Ichhapurti which seemed so far far away.

They sped down the village streets and on to the track that led to the unholy woods. It didn't cross their minds that they could be seen. At that moment they didn't even care. No line would stop them now and they ran swiftly beyond Deja's self drawn boundary. They looked around bewildered. And in the strange silence of the afternoon, only the sounds of their breath greeted them. A soft breeze blew across their faces and sent a chill through their heaving sweating bodies. Even the birds were silent and the trees stood like paralyzed witnesses in the stifling warmth. Then they heard the sound, a soft moaning, a cry – no, a piteous plea for help. Fear kept them rooted to the ground but only for a moment. They rushed toward the source of the sound and reached a recently cleared part of the woods. The sight that greeted them drained the blood from their faces. Deja lay down on the ground, bruised all over, a gaping wound on his head had colored the grass around him a muddy red. His meager clothes were in shreds and the color of blood and they watched in horror as Deja tried to shift his weight and the knife embedded in his side slid deeper. They ran toward the man they called friend and knelt beside him.

'Deja!' Three voices simultaneously called out the shudra's name. 'Deja, what happened, Deja?' Hari cried out.

Birju and Kedar, unable to bear the sight, were sobbing uncontrollably.

Only Hari persisted, angry and defiant, holding his tears at bay with sheer will power.

'Tell us who did this to you. Don't be afraid, Deja.'

But Deja didn't speak. The silence brought Birju and Kedar to their senses and the boys looked at Deja's almost lifeless form.

Birju wiped his tear stained face with his hands and knelt closer beside Deja who was now trembling from shock. His whole body shook and at the sight of the relentless trembling, the boys were besieged by a feeling of anguish and helplessness.

Still kneeling beside him, Birju put his face close to Deja's. 'Deja, can you hear me?'

Even though he still trembled uncontrollably, he managed to nod his head.

'Deja, tell me who dared to do this. I promise you, Deja, we promise to bring you justice. Tell us Deja, tell us!' And even as they pleaded with the dying man, each one of the boys knew the answer.

And Deja looked up to see the tears run down Birju's face once again.

'Don't cry for me, baba.' The three boys gathered closer around him for his voice was a mere whisper. They waited for him to speak and with every passing moment feared that he would never speak ever again. Deja's trembling seemed to abate for a moment and he moved his lips in speech.

The boys bent closer to his face and caught his words.

'What use is justice...to me now, baba? Did I not say...that anything that happens in my life will...be an improvement? At last, I will be free from the bondage of the body.'

He heaved himself on to his elbows in a struggle to sit up but let himself go when he couldn't bear the exertion. He breathed deeply as the trembling started all over again and rendered him incapable of speech. The boys watched as if mesmerized and waited for the shivering to end. Hari got up slowly and walking away, beat his head in a gesture of desperation. Of what use was their companionship to Deja? What had it brought him? Nothing. They had managed to calm their own conscience, but that was of little use to Deja, though he would have disagreed. Even now in his dying moments all they could do was sit and stare. Like the villagers had done every Sunday the past year. For all their courage in coming to see Deja in the unholy woods, not one of them could run to the village for help. Going to the villagers would mean losing the opportunity of being with him in his last moments. For the villagers were sure to laugh at the suggestion that an untouchable's life needed to be saved. And then they were sure to ask how the boys knew of Deja's condition. Not only would they get no aid and leave Deja to die alone, they would belittle whatever little admiration Deja had managed to rekindle in his own community. Birju and Kedar looked at Hari and he knew that the same thoughts ran through their minds.

Deja's trembling stopped once more and he tried to speak again.

'I do not want justice, baba...I want peace. Will you forgive me...if I...if I ask you to do something for me?'

'Deja,' Birju cried. 'Whatever you wish.'

'Can you get someone…from my hamlet to…to conduct my last rites? I do not want to be a wandering ghost after my death…and I will be, if my funeral is not performed.'

He paused to take a deep breath and continued. 'After my death, at least…I want to be able to go home.'

'Yes, Deja. We promise you, your last rites will be performed.'

'Don't go to the hamlet yourself…' Deja said.

'Shut up, Deja.' Birju cut him short and looked through his tears at the little smile that lit up Deja's face.

'Don't ever change, Birju baba. And you both, too,' he said, looking at Hari and Kedar. He paused and with tremors still racking his body took a slow deep breath and continued.

'For a few moments I feared I would die alone. I didn't mind living alone,' he whispered, 'but dying…is different. God has been kind to me…You…you have…been more than kind. Thank you,' Deja said, and folded his hands in gratitude. Seconds later, his lifeless hands fell to his sides and all was silent.

The boys stared at Deja, refusing to believe their eyes. For a long time, Deja lay inert and motionless and then Kedar burst into tears.

So this was what death was like. Every now and then the boys thought they saw Deja's chest heave a little, but soon they gave up trying to fool themselves. Gentle Deja was no more. Yet, his inert body was here, then where was he now? Where had he been *then*? In his now lifeless body, or in his simple thoughts? In the pure smile that touched his eyes, or in his gentle ways? In his unsullied heart or in his quiet words? Where was their Deja now?

A sobbing Birju buried his face in his Mother's lap, as she sat quietly and stroked his hair. When at last he calmed down and the sounds of his crying subsided into an unhappy silence, she held his chin between her thumb and forefinger and turned his face towards her. She looked at the troubled face and for a moment was taken aback by the extent of the anguish in his eyes. This was no trifling grief at things gone awry. Whatever it was that was troubling Birju had stirred his very soul.

And then it came out in a torrent. Deja and how they had befriended him, Vishnudev's vicious lie and treacherous act, Bittu the dog and Deja's very real worry over his only companion. Their happy moments with Deja and the surprising lessons they gleaned from time spent with him. The evil designs of his Father, Uncle and Vishnudev and poor Deja's unhappy fate.

Mother looked on at Birju as he told her of Deja's wish to be cremated according to custom. Deja's story on its own would have moved her to tears, but Birju's despair ensured she would do everything in her power to fulfill the poor man's last wish. And after all she had to make amends. There was little she could do against her husband; it was not in her power to stop him. But, where he had inflicted injustice and unspeakable sorrow, in defiance of his acts she could at least soothe the pain, make amends even if it was too late. And she would. She was a kindhearted woman and many a poor man, remembered her in gratitude. She moved quickly. It was difficult, but with the enticement of money someone was at last found, who was ready to conduct Deja's last rites.

In the dark of the night, Birju, Hari and Kedar met at the edge of the woods and wended their way silently to the clearing, where they were told the man from Deja's hamlet would be conducting his last rites. They moved quietly as they neared the place and heard sounds of activity. In the moonlit night they stayed in the shadows amongst the trees and looked on at the sole man who had agreed to conduct Deja's last rites. Deja's lifeless body, now covered with a white cloth that covered his face but left his ankles exposed, lay by a pile of logs.

They watched in dismay as the man callously heaved the body of the man they had befriended, onto the few logs of wood, and proceeded to place a few branches over the body.

Then, he squatted down on the ground, busying himself with a small pile of twigs. Soon, the man's profile was lit up by leaping flames that reared their fiery heads under his hands and painted the adjacent darkness in orange and gold. The man got up and moved to the small bundle that he had deposited some distance away from the site of his work. He rummaged through the articles and then at last drew out a small bottle and a long piece of cloth that he proceeded to tear into smaller pieces. The man's movements seemed to grow more and more incomprehensible to the three friends. Then at last taking a long piece of the cloth, he got up and doused it with some liquid from the bottle. They waited with bated breath, for in their hearts they sincerely desired to be a part of Deja's funeral. Even if they could only do so in hiding. They watched as the man moved towards the small fire and held the cloth to it. It caught fire in an instant, and trailing the fiercely burning rag on the ground the man walked slowly towards the funeral pyre.

The boys stared in traumatized disbelief, as the man held aloft the flaming rag and made ready to fling it on the pyre.

In the stillness of the night, the agonized cry sounded like a scream from the depths of hell. Fear immobilized the man, as his ears picked up the eerie sound and his eyes simultaneously caught sight of a figure rushing out from among the trees, towards him.

'Stop, you devil.' Birju screamed. 'Stop!' And in one fierce unexpected motion that took even the aggressor by complete surprise, Birju savagely head-butted the man on his chest and watched as he fell to the ground. The rag burned steadily on the ground for a few seconds before dying out with the fire. Hari and Kedar came running behind Birju and looked on in bewilderment at the scene. For a moment the thought crossed Kedar's mind that this moment surely marked the onset of lunacy in Birju. He watched as the man, now over his initial shock, tried to get to his feet. Then recognizing the boys, he changed tracks midway and folding his hands, squatted in the untouchables' habitual pose of deference. The look of terror returned to his eyes and he put shaking hands to his head and pulled at his hair.

'What have I done to deserve this, baba?'

The boys were caught off guard in the wake of the man's response. Hari stared in bewilderment at the petrified figure but soon figured out why the man was so distraught. For the second time in Ichhapurti's history, an untouchable had defiled a Brahmin with his touch. Birju had unwittingly replayed the scene of two years past and the poor man feared for his life.

Hari whispered to his friends as the man continued to moan in his fear. Birju and Kedar nodded in comprehension.

'What were you doing with that rag?' Birju asked the man.

'Baba, I was only doing my duty. I was asked to perform the last rites for the madman and that is all that I was doing.'

'Last rites? Is the flaming rag indispensable to your community's last rituals?'

The man shifted nervously on his haunches from one foot to another, and averted the gaze of the three furious boys.

'Speak up, man.' Hari spoke through gritted teeth. 'Speak up or we promise you a future that will make Deja's fate seem like a godsend.'

'No,' the man begged. 'I beseech you, forgive me. But the madman had brought notoriety to our caste. No one was ready to perform his last rites, after all he was an outcast, a pariah. I agreed only because I was coerced into doing it. But I do not wish to desecrate myself by lighting his pyre the traditional way. He doesn't deserve it…'

'And you think you do?' Birju thundered. 'Deja suffered for no fault of his and I'm sure you are in no doubt that a mere word from any one of us is enough to deliver you to a common calamity.'

'No, no baba,' the man cried, folding his hands and looking with fear-filled eyes at each one of the boys. 'Do not be so harsh upon this mere servant. I shall do as you wish. I shall do your bidding for as long as I live, I swear upon all that is holy. Only forgive me, I am but a wretched creature. Spare my life, my lords. Spare my life.'

'Will you do as we say?' Birju asked.

'May God dispatch me to hell if I do otherwise. I shall only do as you say.'

'It is in your interests to obey us. Leave! Move, this instant and get back to your hamlet.' Birju spoke with quiet confidence and held up a hand to stop his dumbfounded friends from intervening. 'Say what you want to your clan, but if you dare to breathe a word about seeing us here…,' Birju's voice was suddenly unrecognizable in its harshness. 'If you dare to even dream of it, I promise you a retribution so swift and so terrifying that down the ages, your name will be remembered in your hamlet as an example of where a shudra must never venture. In thought, or in deed.'

The man's eyes shone in anticipation of freedom and in disbelief, at the prospect of being let off so lightly. He clasped his hands to his chest and beat it softly. 'You are kind, baba. This creature will never forget your benevolence and your kindness. I will never dare to speak of what transpired tonight for I know the results of the act, were I fool enough to undertake it. From this moment on I will not even recognize you if we come face to face. Thank you, baba. Thank you. I am fortunate to have…'

But Birju could suffer the ingratiating voice no more. 'Be gone, man,' he said. 'Flee, before I change my mind.'

That was all the encouragement the man needed as he got up, folded his hands, bowed and took to his heels, never looking back even once.

The three friends stood staring at the escaping figure. Soon, he was totally out of sight and still they could not bring themselves to face each other. What had Birju done? Deja's inert body lay on the funeral pyre and the thought crossed a disconsolate boy's mind that for Deja, as in life, so also in death, justice was a long time coming.

Birju was suddenly aware that his whole body had gone rigid and he unclasped his clenched fists and shook his shoulders to fend off the tension that had built up in them.

He looked back to find his friends looking at him with questioning eyes. The air was thick with an awkward silence and the flames from the fire that the man had lit blazed steadily. It lit up the immediate surroundings, setting up a dance of light and shadow in the unholy woods, as if in defiance of the darkness that had permeated their hearts.

'What now, Birju?' Hari asked. 'You've let your temper run ahead of you once again. What are we to do now about Deja?'

'Birju,' Kedar almost wailed. 'We can't even go back and ask someone from the hamlet to come here now. We've lost the one man who was willing to perform Deja's rites.'

Birju looked from Hari to Kedar and then at the funeral pyre that stood ready for its fiery fate.

The two boys waited for their friend to respond and after what seemed like ages, Birju sat down on the ground and gestured to his friends to do the same. He sat quietly for a long time before speaking.

'I don't know what you will say to this, but I have made up my mind.' He took a deep breath before going on, his gaze burning into the eyes of his friends. 'I've decided… I…I am going to light Deja's pyre.'

A cry of shock and disbelief escaped the two listeners. Kedar was almost paralyzed with horror. Birju *had* gone mad after all. Hari quickly regained his composure and tried to dissuade Birju.

'We've done all we could for Deja, Birju. There's no need to get entangled in another complication. After all, he's no more. What happens to his lifeless body will matter little to him now.'

'But it matters to me, Hari.' Birju's voice was calm but defiant. 'You don't have to stick with me on this. I…I'll manage on my own.'

'But, Birju…'

'No, Hari.' Birju interrupted. 'Remember Deja telling us that his identity meant everything to him? That not being accepted as one of his people meant he was little better than the unhappy dead who cannot find solace in this world or the next?'

'But Birju, you believe in no such thing.'

'Yes, but Deja did. What is the lighting of a funeral pyre, Hari? A homecoming for the dead, the return of dust to dust. Why must I fear something that I know will bring peace to Deja and cost me nothing? Even when he was dying that was all that mattered to him, and *we promised him* his last rites would be performed. It troubled him day and night, you know it. I don't know about the two of you,' Birju said, looking unhappily at his friends before turning away, 'but I cannot spend the rest of my life thinking I failed Deja. We did little to bring him justice in his lifetime, Hari, in spite of knowing the truth. I will not let him suffer the same fate in death.'

And so the three friends sat huddled together, the thread of friendship that bound them testing its resilience on unfamiliar territory.

For a long time, the boys said nothing and at last Birju stood up.

'You don't have to be here, you know. You're free to go away, I…I can understand.'

He moved forward in the direction of the fire that now flickered a little less rebelliously against its dying moments. Kedar in his consternation at the turn of events, unconsciously shifted his body to squat in the shudra's familiar posture of deference and trepidation, and Hari nudged him lightly to dislodge him from his stance. They trained their sights on their friend once again. Birju picked up a stout length of a branch and held it to the dying flame. Hari and Kedar watched fascinated as the branch claimed the fire for its own and added a flaming brilliance to Birju's countenance.

Gripping the branch tightly to control his trembling, Birju moved towards the pyre and circled it thrice. He had never been to a funeral before but it did not matter. With what little his young mind had been capable of comprehending, he knew that the last rites are not for the dead, but for those still alive. Not so much for the departed soul's rest, as for peace and a sense of closure in the hearts of those left behind. He wished Deja's soul all the peace in the world and God's never ending grace. Gripping the burning branch with both hands, he stood with his back to his friends, ready to lend fire to Deja's remains. It was reassuring to know that Hari and Kedar were still there, even if they didn't agree with his way of thinking. He closed his eyes and took a deep breath as he readied to put fire to the pile of wood on which Deja now lay. He stretched out trembling hands to unite the flame with the pyre. The heat from the flame brought beads of perspiration that ran down his forehead and trickled down his face. Now that the moment had arrived, ominous thoughts swirled in his mind. All that he had studied in the scriptures came back to haunt him. Surely something menacing awaited him in the future for the sin he was about to perpetrate? He knew wise men who had spent years studying the scriptures and still admitted their ignorance of the truth. What was he, a mere boy trying to prove? What horrendous retribution awaited him on the other side?

But his conscience fought back to console him. He was back in his house as an eight-year-old, arguing with his Father. He was listening to his Father berate his cousin in front of relatives for being a blot on Brahmins. Vasu, who was slow in learning and who was happy milking the cows, and repairing anything that was broken, and daydreaming and couldn't care less how God wanted him to conduct himself. And Birju had said, maybe Vasu simply wasn't meant to be a Brahmin. He was surprised at the number of raised eyebrows in the room. He had persisted. After all, didn't Krishna clarify to Arjuna in the Bhagavad-Gita, that no man is born into a caste; that the four castes are born of inherent nature? Why should Vasu be forced to study the scriptures, memorize mantras and behave like a Brahmin if he didn't feel like one? Maybe he'd make a good soldier, or carpenter, or businessman or something else? And Birju was dragged by the ear and thrashed soundly by his Father. 'Any time a situation warrants a dissertation on the Bhagavad-Gita, we'll ask for it,' Father had said. How was it that the scriptures said one thing and people who lived by the scriptures misinterpreted it so easily? After that he had kept his own counsel on things he easily identified as being in variance with reality. He realized too, that elders simply refused to comprehend that which forced them to change. They clung to their ancient beliefs and values because they promised continuity and permanence and freed them from the task of thinking for themselves. Change was what they were really afraid of. Their old values, those stifling nomenclatures which had been handed down to them like ill-fitting cast-offs mattered more to them than the truth. What would they clothe their empty lives with once they decided to change?

He thought of the question that had nagged him the night Deja was exiled. If taking a Brahmin life was the worst sin one could incur, then surely to save a Brahmin life must count as an act of merit? Why then had Deja suffered? Why did the scriptures promise one outcome and abide with the eventuality of another? Why, why, why? The sweat that made its way down his forehead mingled with the tears in his eyes. WHY? The word pierced his very soul as he stood still, mesmerized by the flaming branch in his hand and as if in response to a boy's fervent quest for truth, the answer came to him in a moment of complete clarity. It was true. Man is what he is by virtue of his thoughts and his deeds. A man reveals his true self in his conduct towards the wretched, the less fortunate. The scriptures spoke the truth after all. What a man makes of himself has nothing to do with where he was born. The man who wields his tongue like a sword, only to kill a man's spirit and therefore his sense of self, is worse than the butcher who slaughters voiceless creatures. The butcher has the defense of his calling, to release him from the moral consequences of his actions. The slayer of spirit has no such justification. He is the real slaughterer, the true assassin. Vishnudev was no Brahmin. Neither in thought, not remotely even, by virtue. He was born into a Brahmin family. That was true and that was all he had in his favor. In conduct, for all the advantages of a Brahmin upbringing, he could easily pass for a representative of the very people he berated. Deja had not saved a Brahmin life, after all. He had merely helped extend the lifespan of a man who masqueraded as one. And he had paid for it. If the truth was to be admitted, then Deja was the only one who had acted, without being aware of it, like a true Brahmin. What could be more fitting then, that a Brahmin boy was to light his pyre?

The load in his heart was lighter but Birju found himself shaking uncontrollably. It was only with immense effort that he shook off the feeling of dread. As if in a dream, he moved closer to the funeral pyre and closing his eyes, slowly stretched out still trembling hands to light the pyre. He almost dropped the burning branch in his untold grief, only to find his nervous grip steadied by a pair of strong hands. He opened startled eyes to look at Hari who kept his gaze on the fire and said, 'Wait, while I recite the last mantras.'

And so it was that in the late 1990's, in a small village in India, like so many that dotted this vast country, a little boy faced his fears and grew up almost overnight. Another watched, afraid to step out, onto the lonely road that his friend had begun walking. But courage can be infectious and he had thrown caution to the winds and stepped up to his friend. What threat is a lonely road for two friends who think alike, who are no longer afraid to think for themselves?

Still another watched from a distance. He had not yet gathered the courage to make the journey, but neither had he run away in fear from the truth. Many months ago Birju had said they were partners in crime for being part of the crowd. Now as he watched, he acknowledged he still wasn't as brave as his friends. But at least he wasn't part of the crowd now, wasn't afraid of being a rebel, and that meant he had closed the door on one of man's greatest fears. As he watched the flames from the pyre shoot up into the night sky, Kedar whispered a silent prayer for Deja's soul and felt the load in his heart lighten at the thought that he was no longer afraid of being witness to the truth.

They could see the boats in the distance lazing their way to Ichhapurti's shores. Like they came every six months, for the half yearly festival. The three boys lay on the banks. Birju on his back, one knee crossed over the other, looking for distinct shapes in the abstract clouds that floated dreamily across the azure summer sky. Hari, trying hard to locate an invisible bug that had bitten him and Kedar, keenly observing the diverse crowd that landed on the shore. The chatter of the crowds closed in on them as people disembarked and made their way up the banks. A few stopped for directions to specific locations, while many of them the boys recognized as regular visitors to Ichhapurti. A group of rustic boys, in obvious high spirits threaded their way towards the three friends.

'You are local lads, aren't you?' one of them called out.

'Yes, what are you looking for?' Hari asked.

'Everything actually, it's our first trip here,' the lad answered. 'But first we want to see the madman of Ichhapurti. Been told we mustn't miss him.'

Birju looked away to hide the sudden onrush of tears and Hari quickly replied, 'Haven't you heard…?'

But to his friends' immense surprise, Kedar cut him short. 'The madman of Ichhapurti, did you say? Of course, you mustn't miss him,' he smiled. Pointing the way to the left where the greater number of visitors were already wending their way, he continued. 'That way, my friends. In the village grounds, under the banyan tree, he'll be holding a sermon. All the other madmen are there too, hanging on to every word of his.'

The End

www.ingramcontent.com/pod-product-compliance
Lightning Source LLC
Chambersburg PA
CBHW031440130726
47989CB00003B/1230